FEVER SEASON

FEVER SEASON

ERIC ZWEIG

DUNDURN PRESS
TORONTO

Edited by Michael Carroll
Designed by Courtney Horner
Printed and bound in Canada by Webcom

Library and Archives Canada Cataloguing in Publication

Zweig, Eric, 1963-
    Fever season / by Eric Zweig.

ISBN 978-1-55488-432-2

    1. Influenza Epidemic, 1918-1919--Juvenile fiction.
I. Title.

PS8599.W43F48 2009   jC813'.6   C2009-903255-4

1 2 3 4 5   13 12 11 10 09

| Conseil des Arts du Canada Canada Council for the Arts | Canada | ONTARIO ARTS COUNCIL CONSEIL DES ARTS DE L'ONTARIO |

We acknowledge the support of the **Canada Council for the Arts** and the **Ontario Arts Council** for our publishing program. We also acknowledge the financial support of the **Government of Canada** through the **Book Publishing Industry Development Program** and The Association for the Export of Canadian Books, and the **Government of Ontario** through the **Ontario Book Publishers Tax Credit program**, and the **Ontario Media Development Corporation**.

Care has been taken to trace the ownership of copyright material used in this book. The author and the publisher welcome any information enabling them to rectify any references or credits in subsequent editions.

J. Kirk Howard, President

Printed and Bound in Canada.
www.dundurn.com

| Dundurn Press 3 Church Street, Suite 500 Toronto, Ontario, Canada M5E 1M2 | Gazelle Book Services Limited White Cross Mills High Town, Lancaster, England LA1 4XS | Dundurn Press 2250 Military Road Tonawanda, NY U.S.A. 14150 |

Mixed Sources
Product group from well-managed forests, controlled sources and recycled wood or fiber
www.fsc.org Cert no. SW-COC-002358
© 1996 Forest Stewardship Council

FSC

ANCIENT FOREST ™
FRIENDLY

For Alice, Barbara, and Amanda,
and their experiences in Montreal

CHAPTER 1

"Put your coat on," David Saifert's mother said. "It's freezing out this morning. Hurry or we won't get a seat on the streetcar."

"Honestly," David's father said grumpily, "it was easier to get him out of the flat when he was a baby and you had to bundle him up all by yourself."

David was no baby. It was January 1911, and he had just turned six. He could put his coat on fast if he wanted to; he just didn't like to wear it. "It doesn't fit," David complained. "The sleeves are too short. They get all bunched up behind my shoulders, and the wool's scratchy on my neck ..."

"We can't afford to buy you a new coat right now," his mother explained patiently. "We need you to get the rest of the winter's wear out of this one, so put it on and make the best of it." When he did, she could see he was right. The coat was too small. "I'll see if I can let the sleeves out a little more tonight," she promised while stuffing his mittens over his hands. "Maybe you can help me with the sewing."

Before he could answer, David's father put a hat on the small boy's head with a firm hand. "Let's go."

David grabbed his small satchel, and the three members of the Saifert family left the apartment together. He had been going to work with his parents for longer than he could remember. The family didn't have any more money when he was born than they did now. His parents couldn't afford to pay someone to look after him, so as soon as she was able to go back to work, his mother had to start bringing him with her. Not all poor people were allowed to take their babies to work, but David's mother was lucky. She was a good worker, and Mr. Salutin, who owned the factory, liked her and his father. Mr. Salutin understood that David's parents needed both of their jobs to make ends meet. He was willing to let his mother bring her baby as long as her work didn't suffer. It didn't, and David had been coming to work ever since. He would continue to do so until he started school next fall.

Like most houses in Montreal, the three-storey dwelling the Saifert family lived in on Chabot Street had a long stairway on the outside. It curved in a winding spiral all the way up to the third floor where the family had its apartment. In Montreal, people called these apartments "flats." The man who owned the building lived on the first floor. Another family had the flat on the second floor.

"Grab on," his mother said, holding out a gloved hand for David to grip. "The stairs are dangerous enough for little legs at the best of times, never mind when they're covered with snow and ice."

It took a few minutes for David and his mother to reach the bottom of the stairs. Once they did, they hurried along the sidewalk. They had to catch up to his father, who was already around the corner on Dandurand and halfway to the streetcar stop on Papineau Avenue. David's father always seemed to move quickly. He was tall, but not too tall. Less than six feet. He was thick, but not fat. Muscly and strong. He had to be to work some of the big machines at the factory. Even his hair, which was so dark it was almost black and hung straight from his head, appeared strong somehow. David's hair was a shade lighter than his father's, and his eyes were blue. His father's brown eyes were exceptionally dark and always looked just a little bit angry, even when he was smiling ... which wasn't very often.

A light snow began to fall, and the strong wind made the icy flakes feel like tiny pinpricks that stung David's cheeks as he and his mother scurried along the sidewalk. Scratchy or not, he turned up the collar of his coat to shield his face a bit. When they got to the stop, he turned his back to the wind for added protection as they waited. Fortunately, the city had so many streetcars that the wait was never very long.

Because he was looking the other way down Papineau Avenue, David felt the streetcar coming before he saw it. The ground rumbled as it drew near, and David turned to see the square face of the trolley with its rectangular windows and big round lights. The steel wheels screeched as trolley car number 387 slowed to a stop. David always tried to remember the number of the car.

"Be careful," his father warned as David made the long step up to the first stair that led into the streetcar. Once they were all safely inside, Mr. Saifert dropped the required pennies into the collection box. They hadn't been quick enough to get a seat, but a man sitting near the front offered his to David's mother.

"Thank you," she said as she sat down. She tapped her lap, and David hopped onto it. His mother smiled, which made her eyes twinkle. They were hazel, but always looked a little bluer in the winter and green in the summer. The skin on her face was pale and dry in the cold winter weather, but in summer sunlight her cheeks still got freckles. David knew that when she was a girl her hair had been orange, but it was light brown now. It was still thick and curly, and she needed many long hairpins to hold it up and keep it neat.

Mr. Saifert stood nearby, clutching a leather strap fastened to a bar above the seats. He swayed and lurched from side to side as the streetcar churned along the tracks. David watched his father shift weight carefully to maintain balance. He also glanced out the windows, waiting to see the taller buildings that signalled downtown, and then listened as the driver called out the street names before each stop.

"De Montigny … Saint Catherine … Dorchester …"

The family transferred at Dorchester and caught another streetcar for Saint Urbain Street, which marked the end of their ride.

David's parents both worked at the same hat factory in the garment district in downtown Montreal. His father was one of four men who operated the heavy presses that cut shapes out of large sheets of fabric like cloth and felt. His mother worked upstairs in a room with dozens of other seamstresses, each sewing the cut shapes together like a fabric jigsaw puzzle. David spent the working day sitting beneath his mother's sewing table.

The sewing room resembled a double-sized classroom, except that instead of desks there were rows of tables with sewing machines. Unlike a classroom, though, the room was full of noise as the sewing machines whirred and clattered. The needles moved up and down by means of treadles, wide pedals underneath the tables that each woman pumped with a foot. That way both hands were free so that one could guide the fabric past the needle and the other could steer it out.

The only windows in the sewing room were too high for anyone to see anything. They were only there to give additional light, and not to provide a distraction from work by giving the seamstresses anything to look at. Besides, the women were too busy, anyway.

"We get paid by the number of hats we make," David's mother had told him. "So the women want to get as much done as possible. You're not to disturb anyone."

That had been easier when he was a baby. Then he had spent most of the day sleeping in his bassinet. Even now that he was six years old, he would often fall asleep on the floor for at least part of the day, but he also needed other diversions.

"Have you got your things?" his mother now asked.

David held up his satchel. In it were a picture book, a pad of paper, and some pencils. Lately, though, even that wasn't enough to fill his time, so his mother had begun teaching him to sew using scraps of fabric. Now his bag also contained his own needle and a spool of thread. Certainly, the needle was sharp, but that just taught him to be careful. Even so, it was impossible to be careful all the time.

David sat on the floor to sew, and sometimes he dropped his needle. Usually, it landed flat and rolled to the narrow gap between two of the uneven floorboards. He could pick it up by pinching it with two fingers. But one day the needle landed upright, held by its fatter eye between the boards. David turned to see where the needle had gone, reaching out a hand to support himself. Suddenly, he felt a fiery pain like a bee sting. He had put his hand right on the needle, and when he lifted his hand, the needle was still stuck in his palm, with the thread hanging down. The shock made tears well in his eyes.

"It doesn't hurt too much," he whimpered, trying to make himself brave, which was hard because his palm really hurt. Worse than that, somebody would have to pull the needle out.

He held his palm up for his mother to see, but her eyes were on her work. He would have to solve this himself. The needle wasn't in far, so he closed his eyes, gritted his teeth, and yanked it out. A few drops of blood followed, which he wiped on his piece of sewing fabric. The bleeding ceased after a few minutes. His mother didn't even know anything had happened.

After that there were a few more times when David pricked himself with the needle, but he never again cried at the hat factory.

———

Even though David wasn't supposed to bother other people at work, he would show his sewing to Mrs. Halberstadt. She sat at the table next to his mother. Mrs. Halberstadt had never known a boy who could sew as well as David did, and she liked to teach him different types of stitches. Mrs. Halberstadt would always smile when she saw how quickly he learned them, but some of the other women weren't as kind.

"That boy will make a good wife someday," one of them said. Sewing was considered a woman's job, and many of the other ladies laughed. It was a running joke with them, and each time somebody said it, the others laughed all over again. It embarrassed David.

Later that night, back at home, David's mother had time to fix the sleeves on his winter coat, just as she had promised. "Do you want to help me?" she asked.

"No," David said. "I don't want to sew anymore. I don't like it when the women laugh at me."

"Nobody means any harm by it," his mother said. "They're just having a little fun. Goodness knows, there's not much fun to be had at that job."

"Well, it's not fun to hurt my feelings."

"No, David, it isn't. But don't let it bother you. Think of it this way: They're probably jealous. Just imagine what a help it would be to them if they had husbands or sons who could sew like you do."

"Well, sewing is women's work, and I'm not going to do it anymore."

"That's up to you." Then his mother shrugged, as if to say, "We'll see what happens."

CHAPTER 2

That spring David's father was given a promotion at work. No longer would he be one of the four men running the big machines. Now he was a factory foreman in charge of the whole department. It meant longer hours and more responsibility, but it also meant more money. David's father would now make $15 a week. That would work out to a little over $60 per month, or about $750 for the year. It was enough money so that David's mother wouldn't have to work anymore. She could stay home now like rich people's wives and mothers.

David, of course, could stay at home, too, though soon enough he'd be starting school. "What will you do then?" he asked one morning while helping his mother shop. "Won't you be lonely at home with Daddy at work and me at school?"

"Don't you be worried about that," said his mother. Her excited tone brought out the Irish accent of her youth. "There'll be plenty for me to do once the baby arrives."

David was confused. "What baby?" Then it dawned on him.

"That's right," said his mother, beaming. She actually stopped on the sidewalk and hugged him — even though other people were watching. "You're going to be a big brother. Isn't that exciting news!"

Exciting news? David didn't think so. He'd had his mother's attention all to himself since they stopped going to the hat factory, but a baby would change everything.

"It's true we're all going to have to adjust once the baby's born, but just because some things change doesn't mean everything's going to be different. You'll still be my special boy."

David smiled. His mother always said the right thing, unlike his father, who never seemed to have any time for him. David's mother held out her hand, and he took it happily as they strolled down Papineau Avenue. David's favourite store was Mr. Unger's bakery. He could always smell it long before they got there. On days like today, when the loaves were in the oven, the whole neighbourhood was filled with the wonderful aroma of fresh-baked bread. And Mr. Unger, the baker, knew all his regular customers by name.

"Hello, Mrs. Saifert. Come in, come in. We have some wonderful things today. Bread, bagels, buns. Right out of the oven."

"Just a loaf of bread, please," David's mother said.

Mr. Unger wrapped a soft, fresh loaf in brown paper

and handed it to her. "Three cents please ... Oh, and who's this?" The baker smiled at David. "This can't be your little boy. Look how he's grown!"

David felt his cheeks flush. He was a little embarrassed, but pleased, as well. He knew he was small for his age, but it was nice to have someone make a fuss over him.

"He'll be starting school soon," his mother said proudly.

"I can't believe it. Is this true?"

David nodded shyly.

"Not too old for a treat, I hope?"

David's eyes widened as the baker took a small bun out of a great big oven. The crust was golden brown and perfect, but the bun was so hot that when Mr. Unger gave it to him, David could barely hold it. He had to juggle it from hand to hand, blowing on it, as well as his fingers, until the bun was cool enough to eat. Even when it was, a small wisp of steam escaped when David broke it in half.

"What do you say?" his mother asked.

"Thank you," David said.

Mr. Unger smiled as the boy and his mother left the shop.

After the bakery, David and his mother stopped at the greengrocer to purchase fruit and vegetables. Then they visited the butcher shop for some meat. One thing that David and his mother never had to shop for was milk. It was delivered to the door in glass bottles every day. Deliveries were made early in the morning, and in the winter the milk often froze on the stoop before someone got up to bring it in. In the summer, however, a family had to keep its milk cool in the icebox.

An icebox was like a cupboard for fresh food. It was made of wood but had an upper compartment lined with tin. The upper compartment was filled with ice which, of course, would begin to melt. When it did, ice water dripped down a pipe into the lower "cupboard" compartment. The cold coming off the pipe was what kept the food refrigerated. As the water trickled down the pipe, it dribbled out the bottom and into a pan. If you weren't careful about emptying the pan, a big puddle would end up on the floor.

Like milk, ice was delivered to people's houses in a horse-drawn wagon, but unlike milk, it had to be delivered during the day because the iceman couldn't leave a huge frozen block on someone's porch. When the whole family went to work, the Saiferts had arranged with their landlord to take care of the delivery. But now, as far as David was concerned, the iceman's visits were one of the best parts of being at home.

The iceman came by twice a week. He usually reached the Chabot Street portion of his route in the early afternoon. David watched from the stoop as the iceman employed huge metal tongs to select the appropriate-sized block. Even from his third-storey vantage, David could tell how heavy the blocks of ice were by the slow, deliberate way the iceman moved them. Once he had a block in place, the iceman used a leather strap to lift it onto his broad shoulders. Then, holding on to the ice by the strap, he had to haul it up two flights of stairs to the Saiferts' flat. As he got near the top, David could see the lines of concentration on the iceman's furrowed brow and the muscles bulging in his arms as he struggled to support the load.

When the iceman reached the top of the stairs, David opened the front door. The iceman could only grunt a thank-you as he lugged the block into the kitchen and placed it in the upper compartment of the icebox. Wielding the pick that he carried, the iceman chipped away any uneven bits so that the ice fitted properly. Then he collected his money and left. The trip down the stairs was certainly easier than the climb up.

One day David made up a game in which he was the iceman. He used an old shoebox as his block of ice and filled it with books to give it weight. Then he took a fireplace tool to use as his tongs, but what could he use as a strap?

"Can I borrow a belt?" he asked his father.

"What for? Mine are all much too big for you."

"I want it so I can be the iceman."

"A boy your size?" His father laughed. "You need muscles to be an iceman."

"But I was ... it was only ..." He wanted to say it was merely a game, that he was just pretending, but the words wouldn't come out.

"Maybe you can't be the iceman," his mother said quietly, "but you could do something to help me." She put her hands on her stomach, which seemed to be growing bigger with the baby every day. "It's getting harder and harder for me to empty the water pan under the icebox. Do you think you could do it?"

David wasn't sure, but the doubtful look his father gave his mother made him want to succeed. But carrying water in a wide, flat pan was harder than it appeared. It was pretty heavy, but what was most difficult was trying to keep the pan evenly balanced. If David couldn't keep it flat, the water would start to slosh around, and once it started, it was hard to stop. The water could pour over the sides before he knew it.

"Be careful!" his father barked.

David made it safely to the sink, though, and poured the water down the drain. He hadn't spilled a drop. His mother smiled proudly, but his father hadn't even bothered to watch.

———

In the fall of 1911, David became a big brother. His baby sister was born late in October, but before that, in early September, David started school. He liked learning to read and write, and he seemed to have a good head for doing his sums in arithmetic, but other things about school weren't so great. For one thing, the teachers at Gilford Street Public School were very strict. David had kept quiet at the hat factory, so he'd rarely gotten into trouble for talking. But because he hadn't been around many children before, he had a hard time making friends. After school David usually had to make the long walk home by himself.

When the school day ended at 3:30, David walked home along Papineau Avenue. As the main street in the area, Papineau had a lot of things for him to see and do. First, there was the fire station. When the firemen weren't busy, they would let people see the horses that pulled their fire truck. David had been nervous around the horses initially, but he soon got used to being so close to them. Sometimes he would even save the apple his mother put in his lunch to feed to Buster, his favourite horse.

David was always careful to hold his hand out flat. "They have big teeth," one of the firemen had told him, "and believe me it hurts if they nip one of your fingers." Buster always ate the entire apple. Stem. Seeds. Everything.

After the fire station, David would stop at the dairy. There were no deliveries at this time of day, so all the horses were in their stalls. Here he wasn't interested in horses, but in ice, which was used in the back of the delivery wagons to keep the milk cold. A chunk of ice to chew on made a good treat.

With all the horses in the city, there had to be a lot of blacksmith shops, and there was one right on Papineau Avenue. No matter what the weather — hot or cold, rain or snow — the door to the blacksmith's shop was always open. That was because of the heat from the fire the blacksmith needed to shape the horseshoes.

David liked to watch as the blacksmith put a horseshoe into the coal fire until it glowed red. The blacksmith pulled the horseshoe out of the fire with a pair of tongs and laid it on his anvil. Still holding the horseshoe by the tongs in one hand, he picked up a hammer with the other and began pounding. The piercing sound of metal on metal always made David wince and pull up his shoulders toward his ears. After a few minutes of pounding, the horseshoe was finally the right shape and thickness, so the blacksmith plunged it into a pail of water. A cloud of steam rose up, and the hot metal hissed as it cooled and hardened. Now the shoe was ready for the horse.

The blacksmith lifted the horse's front left foot and held it in place between his knees. Then he used a scraping tool to carve away some of the hoof.

"Doesn't it hurt?" David asked.

"Haven't heard a horse complain yet," the smithy said. David didn't seem convinced, so the blacksmith provided a better explanation. "A horse's hoof is really more like his toenail than his foot. It doesn't have any feeling along the edges. Scraping a horse's hoof isn't much different than a person clipping his nails. It has to be flat and even for the shoe to fit properly."

Once the hoof was ready, the blacksmith used a smaller hammer to attach the shoe with nails — real nails. They had to be long and thin, otherwise they wouldn't hold the shoe properly and could damage the horse's foot. Any nails that were bent, the blacksmith gave away.

"They're good luck," the smithy told David, who kept them in his pocket. Eventually, though, the nails wore a hole through the fabric. David's mother always seemed so busy with the baby that he began to fix the holes himself. Even though his father had a better job, money was still tight after the baby arrived, so it was important for the family to make everything last. That was why he had taken up sewing again.

By the time he started grade three, making simple mends to the family's clothes with a needle and thread was added to emptying the icebox tray as David's job. Although he still said he didn't like sewing — and he didn't want to do it when his father got home from work — he knew he had to do his part to help out.

"But when Alice gets old enough," he told his mother, "sewing will be her job."

Despite his complaints, David was fond of sewing. He enjoyed the satisfaction that came from fixing something that would otherwise have to be thrown away. A stitch here, a stitch there, and a torn shirt was just like new. Better, really, because an old shirt was soft and comfortable. But if David hadn't appreciated the way the women at the hat factory teased him about sewing, it was worse when some of the older boys at school found out.

"Just don't let them bother you," his mother told him. "When they see they can't upset you, they'll lose interest."

"But what if they don't? What if I keep ignoring them and they don't lose interest? What if they never stop?"

"They will," his mother said. "Eventually."

But David believed the teasing would never stop. Finally, it all came to a head in January just after David's ninth birthday. It was the type of cold, clear winter morning that made noses run and cheeks redden.

David was walking to school when he ran into Sammy, a boy from his class who was his friend. The hard-packed snow squeaked beneath their feet, and their breath formed puffy white clouds as they spoke.

"What's in the box?" Sammy asked. Like David, he was small for his age and an easy target for the older boys. He wore wire-rimmed glasses that he was always pushing back up his nose.

"Cupcakes."

"Cupcakes?"

"My mother baked them. It was my birthday yesterday."

"Oh, yeah," Sammy said. "January 12."

No one ever made a fuss about birthdays, so David didn't mind that Sammy hadn't remembered. Only rich people had birthday parties. Still, David seemed glum and Sammy knew why. The reason was coming around the corner as they neared the schoolyard.

"Oh, no," Sammy groaned. "It's Kevin Bull."

The name fitted the boy perfectly, and hearing it made David's stomach lurch.

"Just keep walking," Sammy whispered. "Maybe he won't see us until we get inside the fence."

But the bully did.

"Hey, Momma's Boy. Whatcha got in the box?"

David didn't answer. He just kept walking. If he could get through the gate, Kevin wouldn't risk making trouble on school property.

"Hey!" Kevin hollered, more angrily this time. "Dincha hear me, Momma's Boy?" He caught up to David and shoved him from behind. "I said, what's in the box?"

Fear flashed inside David, but he tried not to show it. He turned away, intending to continue walking, but some of Kevin's friends blocked his path. David and Sammy were surrounded. Now there was no choice but to tell them what he was carrying.

"Cupcakes, huh?" Kevin Bull snatched the box from David's arm. "You bake 'em yourself, Momma's Boy?"

The bully's friends laughed.

"His mother made them," Sammy said, sticking up for David.

Kevin glared at Sammy. "No one's talkin' to you, Jew Boy." Then he smirked at David and the cupcakes. He took some of the small cakes out of the box and passed them to his cronies. They stuffed them in their mouths greedily. It seemed as many crumbs fell to the ground as were swallowed, but Kevin's friends didn't care.

David stared at the bits of cupcake in the snow. "They were for my class," he murmured.

"Tell 'em they were good," Kevin said with a laugh as he and his friends ran off with the box.

Sammy and David finished walking to school in silence, but David was angry. He was tired of being bullied, sick of waiting for the other boys to stop. But they were bigger and older. What could he do?

David was still angry when he saw Kevin outside after school. At first Kevin seemed apologetic.

"Here," he said, holding up a cupcake. "I saved the last one for you."

When David reached for it, Kevin squeezed it in his hand. The cupcake crumbled. Then Kevin ground the pieces into the snow with his boots. The bully's friends laughed. David stared at the crushed remains of his mother's treats. When he glanced up and saw Kevin laughing at him, his face flushed.

"Whatsa matter, Momma's Boy?" Kevin taunted. "You gonna cry?"

But David didn't cry. Instead he charged at Kevin, crashing into him so hard that he sent the older boy sprawling. Then he jumped on him and started punching. It was almost as if he couldn't control himself, as if each of his arms had a mind of its own, swinging and swinging, sometimes connecting and sometimes not. Other kids gathered from all over the schoolyard, forming a circle around the boys and yelling, "Fight! Fight! Fight! Fight!"

David barely heard them. He hardly noticed anything at all. Even after Kevin managed to land a punch that made his nose bleed, David still felt as if he were moving in a dream. It was as if he were watching someone else … until he felt something pulling at his ear.

"Get off that boy! Get up right now!"

David barely heard the voice, but he did feel his ear

being twisted and pulled. The pain snapped him out of his daze, and as soon as he was yanked to his feet, he recognized Miss Graham, the toughest teacher in the school. She wasn't much taller than the sixth-grade boys she taught, but she was wide and sturdy like a bulldog. No one ever talked back to Miss Graham, not even Kevin Bull.

Miss Graham had David's right ear in her left hand and Kevin's left ear in her right, and she continued to twist as she led the two boys into the school. She didn't let go until the boys were seated in the principal's office. By then the blood had almost stopped dripping from David's nose, which was now hurting. Kevin had some puffiness around one of his eyes, but he'd been in plenty of fights before and didn't seem to be in much pain.

"What have we here?" the principal asked, as if he couldn't tell.

"Fighting!" Miss Graham barked. "On school grounds."

Although David had never been in trouble before, he knew what the punishment was for fighting on school property. Everyone knew the principal kept a thick black strap in his office, and just the thought of it was enough to scare most kids into obeying the rules.

The principal spoke to Kevin first. "You know the drill, Mr. Bull."

Kevin got up and held out his right hand, a defiant expression on his face. The principal picked up the strap. It looked like a fat black belt, but it was much stiffer than any belt David had seen. When the principal brought the strap down hard on the palm of Kevin's hand, David saw Kevin's ears turn bright red, but he didn't cry. Not even when the principal strapped him a second time. No matter how much it hurt when it was his turn, David was determined not to let Kevin see him cry, either.

"All right, Mr. Saifert, hold out your hand."

David stood and did as he was told.

"And just let me say how disappointed I am to see a bright boy like you in my office. But if you're going to act like an animal, you're going to be treated like one." The principal brought down the strap across David's palm.

The pain was immediate, and David jerked his hand back. The skin was already turning bright red where the strap had struck. He fought back tears with all his might. Kevin wasn't going to see him bawl. Thankfully, the principal didn't strap him again.

"Now go home," the principal told him. "And don't let me see you in here again."

CHAPTER 3

David's mother could tell right away that he'd been in a fight. It was obvious from the dried blood on his face. Also, his right eye was going black. But she didn't seem angry, only concerned.

"Are you all right?" she asked.

David nodded slowly. Neither his nose nor his hand hurt much anymore. The long walk home in the cold had dulled the pain.

"Well, come over to the sink and we'll get you cleaned up."

David's mother ran some warm water over a face cloth, then dabbed it gently under his nose. The water made the dried blood glisten.

"Daybo gots a boo-boo?"

Although his thawed-out face was starting to hurt again, David couldn't help but smile at his little sister's baby talk.

"That's right, Alice. David's hurt himself, but Mommy's going to make it all better."

Alice clapped her pudgy little hands. Then she looked

serious again. "Dolly gots a boo-boo, too." She held up her little rag doll to show that one of its button eyes was hanging by a thread.

David groaned. He didn't want to sew it up for her. Not now.

"Dolly will have to wait her turn," their mother said. "Mommy will fix her boo-boo when she's finished fixing David's. Why don't you put Dolly in bed like a good little nurse and wait in the bedroom for me?"

Alice toddled off to the room she now shared with her brother, leaving David and his mother alone in the kitchen.

"One of the older boys from school?"

David nodded.

"Do you want to talk about it?"

"Not really." David didn't want her to know what had happened with the cupcakes.

David's mother chipped off some ice from the block at the top of the icebox and wrapped the pieces in a towel. She gave it to David to put on his eye. "Maybe you should talk to your father."

He shook his head. That sounded like a bad idea. His father already thought he was puny and weak. All he would do was make David feel worse. But he'd notice the black eye. "Couldn't we just tell him I got bumped by a horse at the blacksmith's?"

His mother sighed. "I'll talk to him. Tonight. After you're in bed."

David nodded. If his father had to know that bullies had picked on him, then he'd rather his mother did the telling.

That night, when he was supposed to be asleep, David carefully pushed open the door to his bedroom. Although the squeal of the hinges sent shivers down his spine, nobody except David heard it. He could see light coming from the space under his parents' door, and he could make out the sound of his mother's voice. Quietly, he crept down the hall to listen.

"Of course not," he heard his mother say. "I think he needs to spend some time with you, but is he old enough?"

"There's no age limit," his father said.

"But it's so rough. Do you think it's all right?"

"I wouldn't have said so if I didn't. Besides, I think it'll do him some good. All he seems to know about are women's things. This will give him and this boy something in common they can talk about."

"I hope you're right."

One of his parents must have turned off the light after that, because David suddenly found himself in the dark. Waiting silently until his eyes adjusted to the lack of light, he tiptoed back to his room. What would do him some good? And what in the world could possibly give him anything in common with Kevin Bull?

———————

The next evening David's father took him to a hockey game. Even though David had never been to a game before, it was impossible to live in Montreal without knowing at least a little about hockey. People who had skates could use them on the snow-packed streets in the winter, and they played pickup games in lanes and alleys. Small cards showing coloured pictures of hockey players were given away in packs of cigarettes, and many fathers gave them to their sons. David had seen boys trading them at school, but he'd never been very interested in hockey. Obviously, a lot of people were, though, because as soon as David and his father stepped off the Sherbrooke streetcar, they were swept up in a huge crowd heading down Wood Avenue to Saint Catherine Street.

The people in the crowd weren't really pushing, but they couldn't help bumping into one another as they made their way along the narrow sidewalk. Street lights cast only a dim glow, but ahead the entrance to Westmount Arena was bathed in light, and David could see excited faces. He found himself getting enthusiastic, too, as he walked among the noisy gathering. But David and his father went right past the main entrance.

"We have to find someone on the other side," his father told him. He almost had to shout to make himself heard. "Take my hand. I don't want us to get separated."

David had to hold tight as he and his father made their way against the flow of people. He wondered how they were ever going to pick one person out of the crowd, but his father knew what he was doing. There were a lot fewer people once they finally turned the corner, and David's father had no trouble locating the man he was looking for.

"*Salut!*" the man said.

"*Bon jour, Henri.*"

"*Vous venez pour voir les Canadiens, eh?*"

"*Mais oui,*" David's father said. "*Je préfère la façon qu'ils jouent.*"

David couldn't understand what they were saying, but his father had told the man he liked the way the Canadiens played. Most English hockey fans in the city preferred the Montreal Wanderers, the city's other professional team.

"And 'oo's this young fella with you?" the man asked.

"*C'est mon fils, David.* David, this is Henri Leduc."

Henri shook David's hand. His grip was too strong and his breath smelled like cigarettes. "Quite a shiner you got dere, kid. You a hockey player?"

David shook his head.

"C'est sa première partie," his father said.

Henri grinned. "His first game, eh?"

"If we can get tickets ..."

Henri looked around slowly. "The Bulldogs are Stanley Cup champions ... but for you, my friend ..." He pulled out two tickets from inside his coat. "'Ow 'bout some seats near centre ice?"

"Combien?" David's father asked.

"Five dollars for da pair."

David's father glanced at the tickets. "They're in the last row, and they sell for fifty cents apiece at the box office."

"*Oui*, but da box office is sold out, no? And I could get five dollars for each of these tickets to see the Bulldogs."

Five dollars was a lot of money, but David could tell from the expressions on their faces that what Henri had told his father was true. Mr. Saifert agreed to pay.

"*De rien*, Mike. Enjoy the game, kid!"

David waved at Henri, then he and his father rejoined the crowd making its way into the Arena lobby. Mr. Saifert recognized some of the other men inside and spoke to them in French, as well. David just stared. He hadn't known his father could speak the language.

"A working man in this city has to speak some French," his father explained. "Only rich businessmen can get by without it."

It had been cold out, but it was warm inside the Arena, so David started to unbutton his coat.

"Keep it on," his father told him. "And your hat and gloves, too. The lobby's heated, but the rink isn't. It's got to be cold or the ice would melt."

His father was right. It was almost as cold inside the playing area as it had been outside. Even bundled up in winter clothes, it took a little something extra to stay warm while sitting in the seats of a hockey rink.

"What are those people holding?" David asked.

"Baked potatoes," his father told him.

David laughed.

"It's true! A hot potato can keep your hands warm all game. It's too bad we live so far away, or I'd have had your mother make some for us, too."

Fortunately, the Arena rented blankets for people to use during the game. They cost twenty-five cents. David's father paid for one and spread it across both of them when they sat in their seats. Being in the last of the Arena's twelve rows, they were pretty high, but they were near the centre so the view was good. David had never seen so many people in one place before. There were enough seats for six thousand people, and space for several thousand more in the standing-room sections. As the time neared eight o'clock, the fans got restless. Some stamped their feet, others clapped their hands. Many hollered French words

David couldn't understand, but he sensed the passion and joined in. Then, just when he thought it couldn't possibly get any louder, the Canadiens hit the ice and the rink exploded in cheers. David jumped to his feet with the others and greeted the hometown heroes.

"That's Georges Vézina!" his father shouted, pointing at the stone-faced man with the leg pads who was wearing a red, white, and blue toque that matched his Canadiens sweater. "He's the goalie. That's Don Smith and Louis Berlinquette. They're the wingers."

As his father named each Canadien skating onto the ice, David had never seen him so excited. There weren't very many to keep track of, though.

"Teams have six men on each side," his father explained, "including the goalie. They also have two or three spare players, but most of the men who start the game will play the whole sixty minutes. Unless they get hurt."

The last Canadiens player onto the ice was a handsome man with jet-black hair. He got the loudest applause from the crowd.

"That's Newsy Lalonde," his father said proudly. "The captain."

After the ovation for the team's top star, the cheers began to fade. Soon the visiting team took to the ice, but the Bulldogs skated around to only a smattering of approval. However, when the last Quebec player made his way through the gate, the mood at the Arena turned ugly.

"Boo! Boo! Boo!" everyone cried.

"It's Joe Hall," David's father said. "The fans all hate him. A hockey player has to be tough, but Joe Hall's just plain mean. He once got kicked out of a league in Manitoba for his rough play, and I was at the game in Montreal a few years back when he was suspended for punching a referee. The newspapers call him Bad Joe."

"He's got a black eye, too," David said.

"Newsy gave him that shiner in Quebec City last week, so Bad Joe's bound to be out for blood tonight. Lalonde and Hall have been feuding for years."

Just then the referee blew his whistle, and the two teams lined up for the faceoff. Lalonde was first to the puck and pushed it ahead. Then he sped around the Quebec centreman and picked up the puck on the other side.

With Smith and Berlinquette at his side, Lalonde headed for the Quebec end. Ahead of him was a big Bulldogs defenceman, so Lalonde had to go wide around him. Changing direction caused Berlinquette to get ahead of him, so Lalonde dropped the puck back to Smith.

"They can only pass the puck beside or behind them," David's father said. "Anyone in front of the puck carrier is offside."

The fans roared their approval as the Canadiens bore down on the Bulldogs, but they couldn't score. Cheers turned to boos when Joe Hall picked up a rebound and carried the puck out of the Quebec end. There were cheers again when the Canadiens stopped him.

Back and forth went the two teams, the crowd cheering every great play and every tough hit. David was cheering, too. "Come on, Newsy!"

Lalonde picked up a loose puck near centre ice and headed straight for Joe Hall. Smith was at his side, so Hall couldn't give Newsy his full attention. Lalonde looked ready to make a pass, so Hall leaned to his right to cover Smith. When he did, Lalonde kept the puck and raced past him on the left!

Hall swung his stick in anger as Lalonde sped by.

"Did you see that?" David asked his father.

Everyone had.

"Boo!"

"Punition!"

"Penalty!"

But the jeers for Hall quickly turned to cheers for Lalonde as the Canadiens' centre headed straight for the net. David was on his feet with the others. *"Shoot! Shoot!"*

But Lalonde passed to Smith, and the speedy winger scored. Now the applause was louder than ever. Spurred on by their fans, the Canadiens continued to attack. By the time the bell rang to end the period, they had upped their lead to 2–0.

The ten-minute intermission barely gave the fans time to warm up in the lobby, but David didn't care about the cold. He couldn't wait for the second period to start. Shortly after it did, Hall took another swing at Lalonde. This time his stick connected with Newsy's ankle, and the Canadiens' captain fell to the ice. Lalonde said something to the Quebec badman, but the referee got between them before anything could happen. Hall was sent off the ice to a chorus of boos.

The Canadiens didn't score while Hall served his penalty, but they were still pressing when the Bulldogs put him back onto the ice. Smith had the puck and was racing toward the Quebec goal. Berlinquette was hot on his heels.

"Allez-y!"

"Let's go!"

Smith sent the puck across the ice to Berlinquette, who played it behind him to Newsy. Lalonde was racing forward with all his might. He picked up Berlinquette's drop pass and ripped a shot on goal!

The Quebec netminder deflected it into the corner.

"Ohhh!"

With his momentum still carrying him forward, Lalonde chased the rebound behind the net. Hall pursued Lalonde.

"Watch out, Newsy!" David cried.

But there was nothing the centreman could do. Hall shoved him from behind with his stick. The cross-check knocked Lalonde to the ice, and he slid headfirst into the boards. Players wore nothing to protect their heads, and a pool of blood formed on the ice. There were shrieks of protest from the crowd.

"Dehors, Joe!"

"Va-t'en! Va-t'en!"

"Get out, Joe! Get lost! Go away!"

But Lalonde was still lying on the ice when the referee led Hall away, and soon the angry shouts gave way to concerned silence.

"Will he be all right?" David asked.

"It was a dirty hit," David's father said, "but they don't come any tougher than Newsy Lalonde. See, his teammates are helping him up."

The fans applauded as Smith and Berlinquette led Lalonde off the ice. Blood gushed from two cuts on the star's forehead. He sat on the bench for a couple of minutes but then made his way to the Canadiens' dressing room. Hall was sent to his dressing room, as well.

"A match penalty," David's father said. "That means Hall's gone for the rest of the game."

Lalonde didn't return, either. Both players were replaced by substitutes, but the loss of their captain seemed to leave the Canadiens disorganized. Quebec scored twice in the next two minutes, and the second period ended in a 2–2 tie. It looked as if the Bulldogs might win the game, but the Canadiens pulled themselves together during the ten-minute break. They scored twice in the third period and held on for a 4–3 victory that sent the noisy crowd home happy.

It was a long ride home from the Arena, and the streetcar that went along Sherbrooke Street was packed with people who had also been at the game. One man who spoke only French told David's father that it had taken ten stitches to close the cuts on Lalonde's forehead. There were a lot fewer people onboard the next trolley after David and his father transferred at Papineau, and there was almost no one around when they walked the last two blocks to their building on Chabot Street. Not much traffic was left on the road at that time of night, either, but in a few hours the milkmen and their horses would be making their rounds.

"Did you know," David's father asked, "that when I first came to Montreal even the streetcars were pulled by horses? And there was no such thing as cars. I never even saw one until around the time you were born. The sound of the engine used to scare the horses. A lot of people didn't like it much, either."

"I guess cars are pretty noisy," David said.

"But at least they don't poop on the street."

David laughed.

His father smiled. "Race you to the stairs!" he suddenly shouted.

David took off after his father, half running and half sliding along the snow-covered sidewalk as they turned from Dandurand onto Chabot. At the last moment as they reached the flat David skidded past his father and reached the staircase first.

"You win," his father said.

Mr. Saifert's breath was heavy, and the clouds it made in the cold nearly blocked out his face. David was puffing clouds, too. He suspected that his father had let him win, but he smiled, anyway.

Once their breath had returned to normal, David and his father climbed the winding stairs to their flat. It was dark when they got inside. Cold, too.

"I guess your mother's gone to sleep already. The fire's almost burned out."

David's father put two logs into the Quebec heater — a small black potbelly stove that wasn't used to cook but to provide extra heat in the flat on the coldest winter nights. The two of them sat in front of the old stove to warm up before going to bed.

"Did you have a good time tonight?"

"Yeah, Dad, it was lots of fun. But how did you learn to speak French like that?"

"When I was a boy, I worked on a farm in the Eastern Townships. I was only fourteen then, but I was pretty big for my age — the farmer thought I was seventeen — and I was strong enough to do the work. But I had a hard time getting along. I'd only just come to Canada, and we'd done things much differently where I grew up. So I watched the other farmhands and was careful to do exactly what they did. I learned to speak French by listening to them. But I hated it there. The farmer treated me like a slave."

"Where were your parents?"

"My mother and father both died when I wasn't much older than you are now. I came to Canada by myself."

David could see by the expression on his father's face that this was something he didn't want to talk about, so David asked him a question about hockey instead. "Did you really see Joe Hall punch a referee?"

His father nodded.

"What happened?"

"It was four years ago, almost exactly. It was January, but the weather was much warmer than tonight. The ice in the rink turned soft and slushy, and the players were having a hard time skating on it. You could see that they were losing their tempers. Of course, Joe Hall was at the centre of it all, swinging his stick and punching at people. Finally, a fight broke out, and when the referee tried to pull Hall off the other player, he punched him in the face. It took three of his own players to finally pull him off the ice."

"How come hockey players are allowed to fight?" David asked.

His father shrugged. "I don't know. It's always been a part of the game, I guess. But because men like Hall and Lalonde go around beating each other up doesn't mean you can, too. You have to find a better way to handle your problems at school."

———————

The next day David saw Kevin Bull talking to his friends. He could hear that they were talking about the hockey game.

"Then Hall hit him over the head with his stick and Lalonde had to go to the hospital," Kevin said.

"That's not what happened," David whispered to Sammy. And suddenly he realized his father had given him something to talk about with Kevin Bull.

Summoning up all his courage, David told Kevin, "That's not how it happened."

Kevin sneered. "Oh, and look who thinks he knows something about it. How would you know anything, Cupcake?"

The other boys snickered, but David held his ground. "I know because I was there." He still had his ticket stub in his coat pocket and took it out to prove it.

"Lemme see that!" Kevin barked, reaching out to snatch the ticket from David's hand.

David was ready for him, though. He pulled his arm away, and Kevin grabbed nothing but air. Then David flourished the ticket again. "Look with your eyes, not with your hands."

Kevin stared at David for a moment, not quite sure what to do. Sammy seemed scared. David held his breath, but Kevin merely nodded and studied the ticket.

"He was there!" Kevin said to his friends. There was almost a tone of amazement in his voice. "So what happened?"

David released his breath and told Kevin and the others about the game. Every day after that David checked the newspaper for hockey stories. He was especially interested in any about Newsy Lalonde. Sometimes he'd cut them out and paste them in a scrapbook. He put pictures of Newsy and some of the other players on the wall in his bedroom.

Keeping up with hockey news gave David something to share with his father, and it stopped Kevin from picking on him. Everything finally seemed perfect. Then the war began.

CHAPTER 4

The nighttime sky was ablaze with lights. Noise seemed to come from everywhere. All summer long people had been wondering. Now that the war had begun, they wanted to celebrate. Soldiers paraded in the streets, while crowds cheered and sang.

Tromp, tromp, tromp, the boys are marching.
I spy Kaiser at the door.
We'll take a lemon pie
And we'll throw it in his eye.
And there won't be any Kaiser anymore!

"Why's he called the Kaiser?" David asked.

"It's a word like king," his father said. "Kaiser Wilhelm is the king of Germany. Only in Germany they call him an emperor, not a king."

David's father had brought the whole family downtown to watch the soldiers march from the armoury on Cathcart Street and to see the fireworks above the park on Mount Royal. To cheer, not for war, but for king and country. And for victory.

Boom!

A new batch of fireworks burst over Mount Royal, colouring the sky red, blue, and white. Some were just streaks that sped across the sky; others twisted like spirals. Alice squealed with delight.

"Look at that!" their mother cried. "They look like falling stars."

Soon a new group of soldiers strode out of the armoury to the cheers of the crowd. A band began to play military tunes, and the music got right into the feet of the bystanders. Many of them moved out of the mob to strut along the street behind the soldiers. Some of them had obviously been drinking and wobbled as they walked. Normally, it was a crime to be drunk in public, but tonight people laughed about it.

"Why are we going to fight a war with Germany, anyway?" David asked.

"We're fighting because England is fighting," his mother explained. "Canada's part of the British Empire, so when England's at war, we're at war. That's why the Canadian government is sending soldiers."

"But why is there a war at all? What are they fighting about?"

"The reasons are complicated," his father said, "but, basically, England is fighting to protect Belgium from Germany."

"How come?"

"Because when German soldiers started fighting with France a few days ago, they had to march through Belgium to get there. England has a treaty that says it will protect Belgium, so now England's going to help France fight the Germans. So is Russia. The problem is, practically every country in Europe has a treaty like that with someone, so when one of the countries gets involved in something, the others have to get involved, as well. Some countries will be fighting to help Germany, but with so many more countries fighting against them the war can't possible last very long."

"So that's why everyone's saying the soldiers will be home by Christmas?"

"That's right," his father said. "And if that's true, then the whole thing could be over before any Canadian soldiers even get a chance to fight."

"That would be a blessing," David's mother said.

That struck David as a strange thing to say. People wanted to fight, didn't they? Why else had so many signed up to become soldiers in the past few days?

As if to answer David's thoughts, a man stood to address the crowd. Although many men were wearing straw summer hats on this warm August night, the fellow who got up to speak was sporting a fashionable derby.

"I believe," the fancy-dressed man said, "that at this critical point in our history we all must do our part."

The crowd cheered.

Encouraged by the response, the man continued. "We all agree that England has been driven into this unrighteous war and that all British subjects must unite to fight for its interests ..."

Another cheer, but this time the man was sombre. "We all hope and pray that justice will prevail in the end and that our country will come out with honour and glory."

Honour and glory. That was why people wanted to fight. Thinking about it gave David goosebumps. The war was going to be a glorious adventure. Those who fought would bring honour to themselves and to their country.

At least that was what people thought on this warm August night in 1914. By September, more than thirty-two thousand Canadians had volunteered for the army. Few people knew how horrible the war would be. Many really thought it would be over by Christmas. They didn't want to miss their chance to fight.

"My brother, Aaron, signed up," David's friend Sammy told him when school started. "The army pays new soldiers a dollar a day. Poppa didn't want him to go, but Aaron says we can use the money. And the army will pay him for a whole year, even if the war's over by Christmas."

The war wasn't over by Christmas, and after New Year's, Canadian soldiers joined the fighting. Newspapers tried to keep everyone at home up-to-date with what was going on, which was good because it could take a long time for a letter to make it back from overseas. Sammy's family already knew from the papers that Aaron was likely to be sent to France in early February.

"But we didn't know for sure until his letter came yesterday," Sammy said. "Look! It's dated February 9. It says he was boarding a boat for France that morning. That was six weeks ago."

During all that time, and during the six weeks that followed, Canadian soldiers didn't see much action. That began to change by the middle of April 1915.

"The newspapers say Aaron's unit is one of the ones that fought at Ypres," Sammy said. Like most people, he called it *Wipers*, even though the proper French way to pronounce the name of the Belgian town was *Eep*.

Sammy was worried, so David tried to say something positive. "If Aaron was at Wipers, then he's a hero!"

"But what if ..."

Sammy couldn't make himself finish, but it was obvious what he was thinking. What if Aaron had been wounded? Or worse? The newspapers said that thousands of Canadian soldiers had been killed at Ypres.

"You didn't get a telegram did you?"

Sammy shook his head.

David smiled. "If you didn't get a telegram from the army, then Aaron's okay."

But weeks went by until Sammy's family knew for sure. It was June before they received a letter that Aaron had written a month before:

May 4, 1915
Momma, Poppa & Everyone

By now you'll have read about the fighting in the Ypres Salient two weeks ago. That I'm still alive is a miracle. We had nearly a thousand men in our battalion when the battle began. There can't be more than three hundred of us left.

It all started late in the afternoon on April 22 when we saw these strange-looking clouds drifting toward the French position. We'd heard rumours that the Germans had a new weapon, and we knew this must be it — poison gas. Many of the French troops turned and ran. Those that tried to stay and fight were choked to death by the gas. When the clouds cleared, the Germans had a clear path through to our line. There were five of them to every one of us, I swear it, but for two days we held them off. Then the Germans turned their poison gas on us!

The greenish-yellow cloud was coming closer, floating just above the ground. Even from a distance it began to burn our eyes and throats. But then someone started yelling — forgive my language, Mama — "piss on a rag, piss on a rag!" I had a hanky, so I pissed on it and held it over my nose and mouth. Others tore off pieces of their uniform. I know it sounds crazy, and it smelled awful, but there's something in piss that changes the chemicals in the gas. When the Germans marched in behind the cloud, we were still there to fight them!

Those of us who made it through are now resting well behind the lines. I now know why Poppa didn't want me to

fight, but I still say we can't allow those
who would oppress us to carry the day.

> Your loving son,
> Aaron

On and on the fighting went, along a looping battle
line that ran halfway through Europe. Shortly after the
battle at Ypres, a second division of Canadian soldiers was
organized. When the war still wasn't over by Christmas
1915, a third Canadian Division was mustered. Men still
volunteered despite the horrors they had read about,
but no one talked anymore about when the boys might
be home from Belgium and France. Thousands upon
thousands never would.

"We owe it to those who have given their lives to
continue to fight," the newspapers said. "More people will
be needed if we are to win this war, and win it we must!"

Through the newspapers, and more of Aaron's letters,
David and Sammy learned about the life of a soldier on
the Western Front. It didn't sound very glorious at all.

"Aaron says they've been fighting so long on the
same fields that nothing can grow there anymore. He
says bullets from machine guns have blasted the trees so
much that they look like skeletons and that bombs have
burned up all the grass. There's nothing left but mud."

The lifeless, muddy ground between the two armies became known as no man's land. Sometimes the area of no man's land between the two armies was less than a city block. Because they were so close, and because the bombs and bullets made it so dangerous to be above the ground on the Western Front, the armies on both sides had to dig pathways through the mud. These pathways became known as trenches. Soldiers on the front line lived in these trenches.

"Aaron says they're full of rats and lice," Sammy told David.

Although their families were much more comfortable at home, in one way the war was harder on the people who were left behind. At least the soldiers on the front line knew if they were dead or alive. Their loved ones didn't. Every day parents like Sammy's didn't know whether to be proud or sad. In other homes women wondered if they were wives or widows.

Yet in many ways life at home continued unchanged. Children still had school to attend. Mothers still had households to take care of. Fathers still had jobs to do, though because so many men were overseas, women across the country were starting to do jobs that used to be considered men's work. There were still hockey games, too, but it was much easier to get tickets at the box office now. In fact, for just $1.25 apiece — a total that was half what he had paid Henri the first time.— David's father was able to buy two seats in the third row for a game between Quebec and Montreal in February 1916.

"They aren't drawing crowds like they used to," David's father said. "A lot of the men who used to go to games are soldiers now."

So were some of the men who once played the games, but not enough for everyone. David had seen angry letters in the newspapers, and just outside the Arena, someone had stuck up a recruiting poster for the army. On one side it showed a soldier fighting all alone. On the other side there was a crowd watching a hockey game. The words said: WHY BE A MERE SPECTATOR HERE WHEN YOU SHOULD PLAY A MAN'S PART IN THE REAL GAME OVERSEAS?

"There are a lot of people who don't think men should be paid to play hockey when others are fighting and dying in the war," David's father said. "But since some of us have to stay at home, at least it's nice to be able to read about sticks and pucks every now and then instead of always rifles and mud."

Although the crowd inside the rink was much smaller than before the war, the fans still let Joe Hall have it when he came out onto the ice with his Bulldog teammates. David joined in the chorus of boos.

A few minutes later the referee blew his whistle and called for the teams to line up for the faceoff. Newsy

Lalonde was slow to take his position. He was waiting for the Bulldogs' centre to get tense and edgy. Finally, he took his position, and when the referee dropped the puck, Lalonde's stick snapped forward like a serpent's tongue. He drew the disk behind him and spun around to get it.

"Come on, Newsy!" David shouted as the Canadiens' captain controlled the puck and turned toward the Quebec end. On his right side was Didier Pitre. On the left was Jack Laviolette. The blazing speed of the three Montreal forwards had prompted newspapers to dub the entire team "The Flying Frenchmen."

Using Laviolette as a decoy, Lalonde drew the Quebec defence to the left.

"Pitre! Pitre!" the players on the Montreal bench hollered.

Lalonde's manoeuvre had opened up the right side, and he slipped the puck across to Pitre. The burly forward bore down on the Bulldogs' net, then, with a quick flick of his wrists, fired a shot that just missed the far side of the net. The puck boomed off the back boards.

"No wonder they call him Cannonball!" David cried.

The rebound from Pitre's powerful shot bounced out in front, but the Quebec goalie swatted the puck into the corner. Lalonde chased after it and circled behind the net, searching for an open teammate.

Laviolette dashed into position for a pass. David saw

him tapping his stick on the ice, calling for the puck, but before Lalonde could make the play, Hall pushed him into the boards. The hit was clean this time, but the crowd screamed, anyway. David noticed the referee watching the two enemies glaring at each other, but nothing happened.

"Looks like they're going to stick to playing hockey to-night," said a man who was seated next to David's father.

Throughout the first period Lalonde led the Canadiens on the attack, only to be turned back by Hall and the Bulldogs.

"When he chooses to play by the rules," the man next to them said, "Hall's one of the best defencemen in hockey."

Finally, Lalonde got the better of him, beating Hall with a burst of speed and then setting up Pitre for the game's first goal. Newsy tapped his teammate on the butt with his stick, then mussed his hair with a gloved hand as they skated to centre for the faceoff. Just over a minute later, Pitre scored again, and the Canadiens took a 2–0 lead into intermission.

Because the pace of the game was so fast, both teams used their substitute players more than was usual during the second period. This seemed to help the Bulldogs, who scored three times to go ahead. However, with all the regulars back on the ice to open the third period, Pitre scored again and the game was even. Thanks to some great saves by goalie Georges Vézina, the score was still 3–3 at the end of sixty minutes.

"Overtime!" David said excitedly as the two teams switched ends and prepared to break the tie.

Because he had been on the ice more than anybody, Newsy Lalonde was on the bench when the overtime period began. Amos Arbour, his replacement, lined up to take the faceoff instead.

Arbour proved faster to the puck than the Quebec centre, but instead of drawing it behind him he pushed it forward. Then he sped ahead to control the loose rubber. He had only taken a few strides forward when Hall came rushing toward him. But Arbour was ready for him. He slipped the puck over to Pitre just before Hall could reach him, and when they collided, it was Bad Joe who fell to the ice.

The crowd roared its approval and continued to shout as Pitre outraced the other Quebec defenceman along the side boards. Hall scrambled to his feet and chased after Arbour to keep him covered. Another player had Laviolette tied up. With no one to pass to, Pitre cut in toward the net.

"Shoot! Shoot!" the crowd cried.

But Pitre continued to hold on to the puck as he moved across the front of the goal.

"He's waiting too long!" David shouted.

And it seemed that Pitre had ... until the Quebec goalie finally moved with him. When he did, Pitre struck instantly, whipping a shot to the far side. The netminder reached out with a padded hand, but he wasn't fast enough to stop a cannonball.

The puck bulged the twine in the corner of the net. Pitre had his fourth goal of the night. The Canadiens had won the game!

But just as the referee was raising his arm to signal the goal, Hall took a swing at Arbour. The young Canadiens player wasn't even looking. Hall was about to punch Arbour again when Laviolette stepped in his way.

"You want some, too?" Hall growled, and he reached out to grab Laviolette. Within seconds the other players on the ice had gathered around, pushing and shoving at those on the other team. It took a while for the referees to get things under control, and when they did, a line of policemen formed at the gate to make sure there was no more trouble on the way to the dressing room.

"It doesn't require much bravery to hit someone when he isn't looking," said the man beside David's father. "If Hall wants to fight, he should go over to France."

But Joe Hall didn't go to France.

David's father did.

CHAPTER 5

ATTESTATION PAPER

CANADIAN OVER-SEAS
EXPEDITIONARY FORCE
QUESTIONS TO BE PUT BEFORE
ATTESTATION

1. What is your name?
    Michael Saifert

2. In what Town, Township, or Parish,
    and in what Country were you born?
    Lodz, Poland

3. What is the name of your next-of-kin?
    Maude Saifert (Wife)

4. What is the address of your next-of-
    kin?
    1960 Chabot St., Montreal

5. What is the date of your birth?
   <u>Sept. 26, 1879</u>

6. What is your Trade or Calling?
   <u>Factory Worker</u>

7. Are you married?
   <u>Yes</u>

8. Do you now belong to the Active Militia?
   <u>No</u>

9. Have you ever served in any Military Force? If so, state particulars of former service
   <u>No</u>

10. Are you willing to be attested to serve in the Canadian Over-Seas Expeditionary Force?
    <u>Yes</u>

DECLARATION TO BE MADE BY MAN ON ATTESTATION

I, <u>Michael Saifert</u>, do solemnly declare that the above are answers made by me to the above questions are true, and that I am willing to fulfill the engagements by me now made, and I hereby engage and agree to serve in the Canadian Over-Seas Expeditionary Force, and to be attached to any arm of the service therein, for the term of one year, or for the remainder of the war now existing between Great Britain and Germany should that be longer than one year.

Date: <u>August 4, 1916</u>
<u>Michael Saifert</u> (Signature of Recruit)

With that you were in the army, as long as you were healthy enough to pass the physical.

CERTIFICATE OF MEDICAL EXAMINATION

I have examined the above-named Recruit and find that he does not present any of the causes of rejection specified in the Regulations for Army Medical Services.

He can see at the required distances with either eye; his heart and lungs are healthy; he has the free use of his joints and limbs, and he declares that he is not subject to fits of any description.

I consider him _fit_ for the Canadian Over-Seas Expeditionary Force.

Date: _August 4_, 1916
James Duplacey (Medical Officer)

DESCRIPTION OF RECRUIT ON ENLISTMENT

Age: _36_ years _7_ months

Height: _5_ ft _11_ ins.

Weight: _179_ lbs.

Complexion: _Fair_

Eyes: _____*Brown*_____

Hair: _____*Dark Brown*_____

Religious Denomination

Church of England _____

Presbyterian _____

Methodist _____

Baptist or Congregationalist _____

Roman Catholic _____

Jewish _____ *Yes* _____

Other denominations _____
(Denomination to be stated)

"We're Jewish?" David asked when he read his father's Certificate of Medical Examination. "Like Sammy's family?"

"Your mother and I aren't religious people," his

father said. "That can happen when you grow up without your family."

"Mom's Jewish, too?"

"No. Her family was Protestant from the north of Ireland. Most of the Irish in Montreal are Catholics. She went to a Catholic church when she lived in the orphanage, but she never felt like she belonged there. She stopped going as soon as she was on her own."

"But you're Jewish?"

"I'm Jewish," his father said. "Or at least I was until I got to the Townships. There were no other Jews on the farm I worked at, and a fourteen-year-old boy can't keep kosher all by himself. Besides, everyone else on the farm went to church on Sunday, and I was expected to do the same. No one ever thought to ask me what my religion was, but even if they had, I doubt I would have told them. I was already different enough. When I came to Montreal, I stopped going to church, but I still haven't been back to synagogue since my family died."

David was quiet, hoping his father would explain. But he didn't. Later, after his father left them for the war, David's mother told him what she knew about her husband's past. "He only told me the story once. It was shortly after we met. He lost his whole family in one night."

"What happened to them?" David asked.

"It was a pogrom," his mother explained. "An attack on the Jews. It began as they were all leaving the synagogue one Friday night. No one in their village would ride on the Sabbath, so when they heard the horses they knew right away. People began to run. Your father was only thirteen, but he was big and strong. But no boy, no matter how strong, can fight against men on horseback. So he ran when he heard the hoofbeats. He left his parents behind with his little sister. They couldn't get away ..."

David's mother was close to tears, recalling the pain she'd seen on her husband's face when he told her the story. "He didn't see what happened, but he knew the men on horseback were swinging their clubs. He could hear the sound of broken glass, smell the smoke rising from the roofs they'd set on fire. It was the worst attack anyone in the village could remember. Maybe they'd only wanted to make trouble. Maybe they didn't really mean for people to be killed. But a lot of people in the village died. There's no way your father could have saved them. If he'd stayed with them, he probably would have been killed, too. Even though he doesn't speak about it, I know he thinks about it all the time. I know he feels guilty about it. I've often wondered if that's why he was so hard on you. If he'd been a small boy like you are, he might not have gotten away."

David's father had never forgotten that night. It was the reason he wanted to fight in the war. "Because maybe," he'd told David's mother, "when it's over, people like my parents and my sister won't have to be afraid anymore."

"I knew he wanted to fight," David's mother told him. "He would have enlisted at the very beginning of the war, but I asked him to wait. Even with his soldier's pay, there won't be enough money for the family. He's arranged with Mr. Salutin for me to go back to the hat factory. In a war we all have to do our part, but I didn't think it was fair to put another child through that, so I asked him to wait until Alice was ready for school."

David understood that he was going to have to look after his sister once his mother began working again.

David's father left for the army at the end of August 1916. He was being sent to the Canadian military training camp at Valcartier, near Quebec City, where he would spend another month or so before going overseas. He'd already been given an army uniform — dusty green pants and a matching jacket. The wool fabric was stiff and scratchy. The uniform had been a bit too big when David's father first got it, but his mother had gone at it with a needle and thread and now it fitted perfectly.

When he polished up the brass buttons, he looked as sharp as any officer, but David's father didn't have the brown officer's belt that draped across the jacket from the shoulder. He was only an enlisted man.

David, his mother, and Alice went to the train station with David's father when he left. There were no parades this time. No fireworks. Two years later and with no end in sight, the war was a grim business now. A small group of soldiers was waiting on the train platform. Alice tried to count them. "One ... two ... free ... four ..." She didn't get very far. She wouldn't be starting school for another week.

Most of the other soldiers at the train station weren't as old as David's father. They were young men like Sammy's brother, Aaron, saying goodbye to parents and siblings. Others were parting from wives or sweethearts.

"I'll write you every day," David heard one woman tell her boyfriend. He could see that she was trying hard not to cry, but a single tear trickled from her eye and ran slowly down her cheek. Seeing it nearly made the soldier cry, too.

"Don't stare," David's mother said quietly.

David turned away and gazed at his father. He looked uncomfortable in the itchy green wool, and the send-off was more awkward than emotional.

"Give your father a kiss," David's mother said, nudging Alice forward.

The little girl gave her father a peck on the cheek. She was nearly five years old, but still too young to understand where her father was going.

"Be a good girl," he said to her.

David was eleven. Too old for kisses. His father shook his hand instead. "You're the man of the house now." Then he got on the train and was gone.

CHAPTER 6

Later it made David feel guilty to think it, but life was good after his father departed for the war. His mother did go to work at the hat factory again, and David did have to look after his sister, but that didn't involve much. One big bonus was that David got his bedroom back once his father left. His sister moved into the room with their mother.

Alice walked to school with David and Sammy. David still didn't really have any other friends at school, but at least Kevin Bull never bothered him anymore. At home David took care of Alice until his mother got home. His sister was usually happy to play with her dolls. Sometimes, if she got bored, David read her a story. Mostly, though, he did his homework. He still had to empty the tray from the icebox, but with his father gone there was much less mending. Soon, though, there was a lot more sewing to be done.

Even with what his mother was earning and the pay the army sent home from his father, money was tight. So David's mother came up with a plan to make a few extra dollars. The people at home were always being asked to sacrifice for the war effort. Mostly, this meant saving food. David had seen the posters all over Montreal. WE ARE SAVING YOU. *YOU* SAVE *FOOD* said one of the signs, and there was a picture of a stern-looking soldier. Another sign read: WELL-FED SOLDIERS *WILL WIN* THE *WAR*.

Other posters urged Canadians to buy fresh fish. SAVE THE MEAT FOR OUR SOLDIERS, these signs said. People were also warned that they could be fined for hoarding flour and sugar. Material for clothing was also important and had to be conserved. Even for the families who could afford to buy new clothes whenever they wanted, mending their old ones became a patriotic duty. But with so many women working while the men were in the army, there wasn't always time for sewing. So David's mother began earning extra money by taking in mending for other families in the neighbourhood. She did those sewing jobs in the evenings and on weekends. With David's help she was able to get a lot done.

David didn't need to feel bad about sewing now. He was doing his bit for the war effort! Even soldiers in the army were issued with sewing kits as part of their gear. Of course, they usually referred to their kits as "housewives" but still … If soldiers sometimes had to do their own sewing, how much shame could there be in doing it at home?

Most nights, after Alice went to bed, David sat with his mother and they sewed together. She had brought home an old sewing machine from the hat factory and used it for big jobs. David did most of the small repairs by hand. Often when they were working his mother told David stories about when she was a girl back in Ireland. One night she told him how she and her brother had come to Canada.

"Your Uncle Danny and I weren't really orphans like your father," she said. "We still had our mother."

David was surprised.

"It wasn't uncommon," his mother said. "It still isn't. Even here in Canada there are many children who get sent to orphanages because their parents can't afford to keep them. That's what happened to our mother. She moved us all in with her father after our father died. Her father had a butcher shop, and our father had worked for him. But a few years later our grandfather had an accident. I never knew what happened to him, but it was bad enough that he couldn't work anymore. So our mother had to take a job as a servant. There wasn't enough money for her to raise her children and take care of her father, too. Then she heard about the groups that sent children to Canada, and she thought we'd have a chance for a better life here.

"Danny was so young, I don't know if he even remembered our mother after a while. She used to write us letters at first. I always hoped that someday she'd come to Canada and we'd all be together again. I used to dream about it. It's hard to believe, but sometimes I still do! When I have those dreams, I'm the age I am now, but Danny's still just a boy."

His mother sighed. David never knew how much his mother thought about her brother, but he could always tell that when she did it made her sad.

"Eventually," she continued, "the letters stopped coming. After Danny got adopted, the people at the orphanage told me that our mother had died."

David never asked his mother much about what it was like to grow up in an orphanage. And though he was curious, he didn't ask much about his Uncle Danny, either. Sometimes he'd look at the stack of letters in his mother's drawer, but he never took the ribbon off to read them. He knew she'd gaze at the half-photograph of her brother, and every so often he'd look, too. As he got older, it was amazing how similar he and his uncle were.

He remembered the first time he'd seen the half-photograph. He was seven years old. It was just a few months after Alice was born. His sister had cried all the time when she was a baby. All she did then was eat, sleep, and cry. And make a mess in her diapers. And wake up the family in the middle of the night.

"I like that Alice cries," David's mother had told him. "I was so worried every time you made a noise. If you cried at home, I was afraid you were sick. And at work? If you cried when I took you to work, I thought I'd lose my job."

"But I was a good baby, wasn't I?"

"You were very good. And so is Alice. She just likes to cry. So did your Uncle Danny." A faraway look crossed his mother's face when she mentioned the name of her brother. It was an expression that seemed happy and sad at the same time. "You know, you're just like him. I've never shown you the photograph, have I?"

David shook his head. His mother didn't talk about her brother very often. He hadn't even known she had a picture of him.

He followed his mother into her bedroom. She put his sister down in her crib and pulled open the top drawer of her dresser. His mother moved aside some of her things, and David saw a stack of letters tied with a ribbon. Beneath it was a small cardboard folder, which his mother picked up. The top corner where it opened was bent, and the cardboard had started to split. His mother opened the folder carefully and took out a photograph. Or rather, half a photograph.

"How come it's cut like that?" David asked.

"It was the only picture we had of the two of us. I took the half that showed Danny. He has the half that shows me. Or at least he had it ..." His mother's voice trailed off, and David thought she might start to cry. "It's been so many years. How could I know if he still has it?"

David's mother handed him the photograph. He took it carefully. "He looks older than me."

"You're right," his mother said. "He's ten or eleven. I don't remember exactly. It was taken a year or two after he was adopted. His new family was very kind to me and would have me over to their house for birthdays and holiday dinners. They just didn't want to adopt a teenage girl."

David studied the boy in the picture, then glanced at himself in the mirror above the dresser. Despite the difference in ages the resemblance was remarkable. Both boys were skinny and a bit small for their age. The shape of their faces was almost identical, and they had the same combination of dark hair and light eyes. "What colour are his eyes?"

"Blue," his mother said. "Just like yours."

David didn't want to ask anything that would make his mother sad, but he was curious. "If his family was so nice to you, how come you never see him anymore?"

"Danny's new father worked for the Canadian Pacific Railway," David's mother explained. "When Danny was twelve, Mr. Embury was transferred to their office in Winnipeg and they moved away. That was just a little bit after I left the orphanage to work at the rooming house where I met your father. I'd send Danny postcards because the stamps cost less, and he'd send me letters. They weren't in Winnipeg very long when his father was offered a better job in Vancouver. Danny didn't want to move again, but it was a big opportunity for Mr. Embury, so they had to go.

"It was very sad," David's mother said, and he could tell from her face that she didn't just mean moving again. "They were only in Vancouver about a year when Danny's father got very sick. He had to go to a special hospital in Seattle, and Danny and his mother moved there, too, so they could be close to him. He seemed to get better, but I guess he never really recovered. He died about a year later. Soon after that the letters stopped coming. After a while, I didn't bother writing to him anymore, either."

As if she could understand what her mother was feeling, Alice began to cry.

"You might not think much of your sister right now," David's mother had said as she had picked up the baby and tried to soothe her, "but I know you will when you both grow older. There's nothing in life as important as family, David. Always remember that."

Now, though, instead of asking his mother more about her family, he asked her questions about his father.

"If his parents were killed, how did he get sent to Canada?"

"I don't remember all the details," his mother said, "but it had something to do with another relative. People in their village knew that his mother had a cousin living in England. Someone wrote to him, and he arranged to have your father brought to London. From there it was easy enough to find a charity that would send him to Canada. That was how a boy from Poland wound up on a farm in Quebec."

"Did he speak with a Polish accent?"

David's mother laughed. "I imagine he must have. But I didn't know him then. That would have been about 1892, I suppose."

"He told me he learned to speak French when he was working on the farm."

"And English, too, I should think. He spoke them both very well by the time I met him."

"When was that?"

"It was in the spring of 1901. Your father had left the farm a few years before that when he turned eighteen. He was twenty-one when I met him, and he already had his job at the hat factory. He had just moved into a rooming house not too far from here."

"And you had a job there cooking and cleaning?"

"That's right," David's mother said with a smile. "I worked there and I lived there, too. That's how your father and I met. We got married two years later."

"And that's when you started working at the hat factory?"

"Not right away, but soon. After we got married,

your father didn't want me to work in the rooming house anymore. We needed to find somewhere else to live, but neither of us had much money. So your father asked Mr. Salutin if I could have a job in the sewing room. I started working there right after New Year's in 1904 ... and you were born a year later."

――――――――

With his father gone David didn't get to any more hockey games. Still, he kept up through the newspapers and with his scrapbooks. The war was definitely having an effect on hockey. Fit, strong men were always needed for the army. Young hockey players were expected to sign up. Many of them did. All the best amateur leagues in Canada had teams of hockey-playing soldiers by 1916. The men would stay in shape by playing hockey, then they would be sent overseas to see action in the war. Still, some amateur leagues had to stop playing. Too many of their players — and even the fans who used to watch — were in the army now. That wasn't just true for hockey. It was the case for a lot of sports. The professional leagues struggled on, but it wasn't easy. Many pro hockey players had joined the army, too. Even the National Hockey Association, the top professional league in the sport, had a team of soldiers during the winter of 1916–17.

David's father had told him it was nice to be able

to read about sticks and pucks instead of rifles and mud. Now there were more stories than ever about the war. They were starting to take over the sports section, too. Practically every day it seemed there was news about a former sports star killed or wounded in the war. All around the neighbourhood David was hearing more and more stories about who had been getting the dreaded telegrams. "We regret to inform you that your father, brother, son, or husband has been wounded." Or worse.

Near the end of the school year in the spring of 1917, David was walking to school with Alice. Sammy was waiting for them as usual at the end of the block. As soon as David saw Sammy's face, he knew something was wrong.

"We got a telegram last night," Sammy said. "From the army ..."

"What did it say?" David wasn't sure he wanted to hear the answer.

"Aaron was wounded in the battle at Vimy Ridge."

David expelled his breath, relieved that Sammy's brother hadn't been killed. "Will he be all right?"

"It doesn't say. It only says he's been sent to a hospital in England."

That could only mean bad news. David knew they only sent wounded soldiers back to England when they were badly hurt. "Do you know what happened?"

Sammy shook his head. "It doesn't say."

———

Aaron was sent home from the war late in the summer of 1917. He was in bad shape, but it was hard to tell. By then the streets of Montreal were filled with broken-down men back from battle. There were men missing an arm or a leg. Others had had parts of their faces blown off. You didn't see them much. They were horrible to look at and rarely went outside. "Compared to them," Sammy told David, "Aaron seems fine." But he wasn't.

"His lungs have been damaged by the gas," Sammy said. "And if you see him without his shirt, his stomach is full of scars. I don't know what happened, but it's hard for him to eat properly." It was also difficult for him to go to the bathroom, but Sammy couldn't bring himself to tell David that. But there was one other thing he did have to let his friend know. "We have to move."

David didn't understand. "Move what?"

"Move away. To live."

The doctors had told Sammy's parents that it would be best for Aaron to recover if he could be somewhere quieter with more fresh air. The family was going to move north of the city.

They left just before school started in September. David never saw Sammy again.

CHAPTER 7

The war was changing everything. By November 1917, it even looked as if there would be no more professional hockey. It seemed that almost every day David read a story in the newspaper saying that the National Hockey Association was going to go out of business. Then, on November 10, it actually happened. The NHA announced it was shutting down. The league was supposed to have five teams that season, but the owners decided there weren't enough players available.

Almost as soon as the old league was dead, though, rumours surfaced that a new one would start. Only four of the old NHA teams would be in it, but no one was certain which four. Everything was finally worked out at a meeting in Montreal on November 26. David read all about it in the next day's newspaper. The new organization was called the National Hockey League, and the four teams in it were the Montreal Canadiens, the Montreal Wanderers, the Ottawa Senators, and Toronto. In the NHA, Toronto's team had been known as the Blueshirts. In the NHL they became the Toronto

Arenas ... because they were owned by the same company that owned the arena they played in.

It had come down to a last-minute decision if Toronto or Quebec was going to be in the NHL. Toronto got the nod when the Bulldogs decided not to run their team at all. The Quebec players were divided among the other teams in the league. The Canadiens wound up getting Joe Malone from the Bulldogs. They also got Bad Joe Hall.

David remembered the brawl at the end of the last game he'd seen with his father. Hall had started it. He'd cut Newsy Lalonde for ten stitches the first time David had seen him. Like his dad had told him, those two always seemed to be fighting.

"And now they're supposed to be teammates?"

David didn't realize he'd said it out loud until his mother asked, "Who's supposed to be teammates?"

"It's nothing, Mom." David reached for the pair of scissors. "Just something in the newspaper."

David knew his mother didn't really like hockey. "Such a violent game," she was always saying.

During the next two weeks, there were lots of stories in the newspaper about Hall and Newsy. At first even the reporters seemed surprised that the two might be teammates. But by the beginning of December it looked as if they really would be.

David read in the newspaper on December 3 that Hall had almost agreed to accept the contract George Kennedy, the Canadiens' owner-manager, had offered him. But Bad Joe was still at home in Brandon, Manitoba, and the Canadiens were about to begin training camp. He wasn't there for the first practice on December 5, but the next day's newspaper said he'd be on his way shortly:

WESTERN WILD MAN TO BE IN CANADIENS UNIFORM SOON

George Kennedy received a telegram from Joe Hall today. It says that the "Bad Man" will leave Brandon on Saturday night. Hall will probably be out for practice on Tuesday with the Canadiens, side by side with his dear friend Newsy Lalonde.

Hall arrived in Montreal by train on the evening of December 11. The next day he was out for practice … and a pack of reporters were there to see what would happen. Nobody really knew what to expect, but everything went smoothly:

NEWSY AND HALL MADE PEACE
AT PRACTICE TODAY

Joe Hall and Newsy Lalonde, long
sworn enemies on the ice, turned out
as teammates for the first time when
the Canadiens held a noon practice at
the Arena. Hall arrived last night from
Brandon and had his first workout with
the champs.

"I'd rather have you with me than
against me," chorused these two veterans
of half a dozen vicious fights on the ice as
they shook hands in the dressing room
today. And they both meant it.

So any problems the Canadiens might have had
seemed to be solved. But the NHL still had troubles.
Even with only four teams, so many players were in the
army that there wasn't really enough talent to go around.
The Montreal Wanderers were the hardest hit. Their
owner had been losing money every year since the war
started. Now, between injuries and army enlistments, they
barely had enough players to make up a team. All during
December the Wanderers begged the other teams to loan
them players. Nobody did. When the season opened on

December 19, only about seven hundred fans showed up for the Wanderers' first game. David could hardly imagine the beautiful Westmount Arena so empty. The Wanderers beat Toronto 10–9, but they lost their next game to the Canadiens 11–2. Two more lopsided losses followed.

Then, early in the morning of January 2, 1918, fire broke out at Westmount Arena. It was thought to have started in the electric wiring in a small dressing room used by the Wanderers. The Arena was built from brick and steel. Many people thought that made it fireproof. However, all the seats were made of wood. The dressing room where the fire started was under the stands, and within a few minutes the whole inside of the Arena was ablaze.

The heat from the fire caused three explosions. The first to blow were the boilers in the basement. They were what kept the lobby so warm. After that the tanks full of chemicals that froze the pipes to make the ice exploded. When David had gone to his first game in 1914, the Arena still relied on natural ice. The pipes to make artificial ice had been added the next year.

After the chemical tanks burst, the force of the detonation blew out the brick walls of the Arena. The steel girders holding up the roof were still standing, but not for long. They were soon so hot that they began to bend. The roof fell in with a loud rumble. Then the flames leaped to the six buildings across the street, but the firemen were able to bring those blazes under control quickly. Still, the heat from the fire broke the windows in many of the homes along Wood Avenue. There was nothing the firemen could do to save the Arena. Within an hour nothing was left but burning rubble.

The day after the fire the Canadiens announced they would move their home games to Jubilee Rink. With only 2,633 seats and standing room for only a few hundred more, Jubilee was less than half the size of Westmount Arena. It did have one advantage for the Canadiens, though. It was in the east end of town where most of their French-Canadian fans lived. Most of the Wanderers fans were English and lived in the west end.

After the fire, the Wanderers made one more plea to the other NHL teams to loan them players. When they didn't, the Wanderers decided to drop out. The league would carry on with just three teams.

———————

About a month after the Arena fire, David and Alice came home from school to find their mother already there waiting for them. She had gotten a telegram. Their father was dead.

For the longest time it hardly seemed real. Eventually, the army sent home some of David's father's things, but there was never a proper funeral. "Body unrecovered for burial," the telegram had read. David was afraid to ask his mother exactly what that meant. He had a pretty good idea, though. His father's body had been so blown apart by shellfire that there wasn't enough left to bury.

Although she tried her best to hide it from him and Alice, David could tell that their mother was sad. She looked older now. There were streaks of grey in her brown hair. But the strange thing for David was that so little seemed to change after his father was killed. He had already been gone for close to two years. David had stopped expecting him to come home soon a long time ago. And there was still school, work, and sewing to help out with. Just as there was before.

By the end of the summer in 1918, it was starting to look as if the war might actually be near its end. More and more wounded soldiers were returning home. David noticed the way his mother gazed at the men in uniform when she passed them on the street. It was as if she were searching for something in their faces, as if the army had made a mistake and one of these men would turn out to be her husband. That was when it finally became real to David. Unlike these men, his father was never coming home.

CHAPTER 8

Soon there was something new to worry about. During the summer of 1918, a different kind of war story was sneaking into newspapers. There wasn't much written about it, so it was easy to miss.

Since the spring, more and more of the soldiers in the hospitals of Europe weren't suffering from battle wounds. They were ill with some kind of sickness. It was like the flu — with a runny nose, cough, aches, and a fever — but it was much worse. Men were coughing up blood, and they seemed to be choking on the fluids that filled their lungs. The disease struck soldiers in England, France, and Germany. Civilians, too. Soon people were sick all over Europe.

Although it was a serious problem, very little about the disease was reported in the newspapers. There was enough bad news from the war already. But Spain wasn't fighting in the Great War. During the month of May, eight million people were sick in Spain. The newspapers there printed plenty of stories about the sickness. As a result, the disease became known as

Spanish Influenza ... or Spanish Flu for short.

Near the end of the summer of 1918, soldiers returning home from the war brought the Spanish Flu back to North America. By now the disease was much more deadly than it had been in the beginning. In late August three sailors were sick with the Spanish Flu at a navy barracks in Boston. Within a few weeks thousands of people in Boston were sick. Most people got better, but lots of them were dying. Soon the same thing was happening in other American cities. Returning soldiers also brought the disease to Canada. It spread everywhere: big cities and small towns, rural farm communities and remote islands. It didn't matter. Anywhere there was air to breathe that air could carry germs.

The Spanish Flu hit Montreal during the last days of September. Some of the stories about the disease were so bad they didn't seem real.

"One of the boys at school has a cousin in Boston," Alice told David on their way home one day. "He says it turns your skin blue. He says some people turn so dark you can't tell if they're white people or Negroes."

David had heard the same thing, but he hadn't wanted to believe it.

Alice's voice dropped to a whisper, her eyes big and round. "He says that blood comes out of your nose and mouth. Sometimes even your eyes and your ears."

David shook his head. That couldn't be true. "He's lying. He's just trying to scare you." But David had heard those stories, too. What if they were true? "Even if it's true in Boston," he told Alice, "the newspapers say the cases here are mild."

But they quickly got worse. About a hundred people died in Montreal during the first week in October. Soon the newspapers were filled with stories about the Spanish Flu, or *la grippe*, as they called it in French. Death tolls were reported almost like sports statistics. People were getting spooked. Something had to be done.

Dr. Boucher was in charge of the Department of Health in Montreal. He decided that the city had to close all its public buildings. Theatres, dance halls, concert halls, and sports events were all cancelled. Schools were closed, too.

"You can catch it from anyone, so I want you to stay inside as much as possible," David's mother told him and Alice. "But fresh air is important, too, so keep the windows open. And if you want to go out, stay on the third-floor landing. I don't want you going down to the street for any reason. And if the iceman comes, or anyone else, don't let them in unless they're wearing a mask over their nose and mouth! And both of you have to wear your masks, too, as long as other people are in the house."

People had been told to wear a mask at all times when

they went out. Police could arrest anyone who didn't. People could buy their masks in drugstores for anywhere from five cents to a quarter. For the people who couldn't afford them — or were too afraid to go out! — newspapers printed instructions on how to make masks at home.

"What about you?" David asked his mother. Offices and factories hadn't been closed. "You still have to go to work."

"Don't worry about me. All the windows are being kept open on the streetcars to keep the air fresh, and the police are watching every night to make sure they get cleaned out properly."

To ensure streetcars didn't get too crowded, most stores had to be closed by four o'clock. That meant shoppers would all be home before other businesses closed for the day. Only drugstores, grocery stores, and restaurants were allowed to stay open late.

"But what about when you're at the factory?" David pressed his mother.

"All the women in the sewing room will be wearing masks. Some of the windows will be propped open, too. And if anyone so much as coughs or sneezes, there's a good chance they'll be sent home."

The weather had been unusually cold and damp for several weeks. Lots of people already had colds. It didn't mean they had the flu, let alone the deadly Spanish Flu, but the symptoms were so similar it was better to be safe than sorry.

————————

The days alone in the flat were long and boring, but David and Alice mostly stayed inside. Dr. Boucher and the newspapers kept saying it was important to breathe fresh air, so they went out to the landing a few times each day. When their mother came home, she called out to them so that David and Alice could go into his room. As soon as she got inside, their mother changed out of the clothes she'd been wearing and put on a simple dress she kept near the door. Then she put her mask and her outdoor clothes in a pot and boiled them to kill any germs. She also put the mail from outside and the newspaper she brought home into the oven for a few minutes. Finally, she mixed up a mouthwash the newspapers said people should gargle: one quart of boiled water, two teaspoons of salt, half a teaspoon of permanganate of potash. Permanganate of potash was poison if you used too much, but it was safe if you were careful. She poured some into a glass for each of them — sharing cups, plates, forks, or spoons was something to avoid! — and they each rinsed out their mouths. Then their mother cooked dinner.

After eating, Alice helped wash the dishes. That was her job, but these days David usually helped, too. At least it was something to do! There was no extra sewing anymore because it was too risky to bring in clothes from other people's houses. If they weren't using a handkerchief when they coughed or sneezed, there could be germs all over their clothes.

Other people obviously weren't being as cautious as the Saiferts. Or maybe it was just impossible to keep the Spanish Flu away from everyone. So many things were closed that the city was like a ghost town, yet more and more people kept getting sick. More than two hundred and fifty people died in Montreal during the second week of October. Almost two thousand more people got sick. And those were just the cases the newspapers knew about. There were probably more. The next ten days were even worse. Nearly a thousand new cases were reported and more than a hundred people died every single day.

The numbers were horrifying, but the speed of the disease was also frightening. Most people who caught the Spanish Flu got better after a week or two in bed. Not everyone, though. Some people lingered for weeks before dying, but others were dead within a few days. Sometimes it only took a couple of hours. A person could be perfectly healthy before breakfast, feel feverish at lunch, and be dead before dinner.

At its worst the disease really was just as terrible as Alice had heard. People's lungs filled up with bloody fluid, making it almost impossible for them to breathe. Without enough oxygen in their bodies, people's skin really did turn blue. There was blood when they coughed, and sometimes it did run out of people's noses instead of snot. Almost no one got better if their case got that bad.

One of the strange things about the Spanish Flu was the people it killed. Usually, the only people who died from the flu were very young or very old. With the Spanish Flu the people who had been healthiest before they got sick were the ones who died. Men and women in their twenties and thirties seemed to be at risk most.

David read in the newspaper about Hamby Shore. He was a hockey player with the Ottawa Senators. Or rather he had been. Shore caught the Spanish Flu from his wife. She got better, but he died. He was only thirty-two years old. Younger people were dying, too. On the same day as Hamby Shore's funeral in Ottawa, Bob Marshall died in Montreal. His father, Jack Marshall, had starred for years with the Montreal Wanderers. Bob Marshall was only twelve.

It was impossible to care for everyone who got sick. Hospitals filled up quickly, so emergency hospitals were set up in schools, orphanages, and armouries. They filled up, too. One big problem was there weren't nearly enough doctors and nurses for everyone. So many medical people had been needed for the war and were still in Europe. Many of the doctors and nurses who were at home to treat the Spanish Flu caught the disease themselves from their patients. Nuns and priests helped out. So did Jewish and Protestant organizations. But there still weren't enough caregivers to go around.

Early on Dr. Boucher had told the newspapers: "The best thing to do when a person is sick is to stay at home and call a doctor." But just a few days later the newspapers were telling people to use their telephones as little as possible. So many operators had become sick it was impossible for the phone company to handle all the calls.

That meant that even though the Spanish Flu was a deadly disease, many people were forced to care for their own sick relatives by themselves at home. Newspapers offered advice on what to do:

> People should be kept in well-lit rooms. Other family members should not enter except when absolutely necessary.
>
> Opening and closing doors set up currents of air that carry germs. It is better to leave the door of the sick room open. Hang a sheet moistened with bleach in the opening.
>
> The person attending the patient should wear an apron with sleeves. The

apron should be removed when leaving
so as not to carry away germs. Wash your
face and hands after touching a patient.

All the linen and other things belonging
to the patient should either be burnt or
boiled for at least fifteen minutes.

There were no vaccines to prevent the Spanish Flu.
There was no sure way to cure it, either. The only thing
to do was to try not to catch it. Newspapers offered
advice on that, too:

Avoid persons suffering from colds, sore
throats, and coughs.
Cough in a handkerchief or behind your
hand.
Avoid cold rooms.
Sleep and work in fresh, clean air.
Eat plain, nourishing food.
Avoid alcohol.
Change handkerchiefs frequently.

———

By the beginning of November, things finally seemed to
be settling down. "We have fewer deaths," Dr. Boucher
told the newspapers, "and I hope the death rate will

keep on decreasing. Still, I advise the public to continue to take the same precautions. It is absolutely necessary to observe these precautions in order to prevent a revival of the epidemic."

November 2 was a Saturday. David and Alice spent the whole day with their mother. Wearing their masks to be careful, they all went out for a short time to shop for food. Later, their mother showed Alice how to work the sewing machine.

"Sit here beside me and pump the treadle," their mother told Alice. "You have to keep it moving smoothly. Heel and toe. Heel and toe. Almost like you're pedalling a bicycle."

Once Alice got the hang of it, their mother placed a piece of cloth under the presser. She hadn't set up the needle and thread yet. First she wanted Alice to get used to moving the cloth with her hands while she pumped the treadle.

"Just push it under gently," their mother said. "You don't have to pull it out the other end. Once you get a rhythm going, the machine practically moves the cloth for you."

When Alice was ready, their mother put the spool in place. It had to be wound carefully through a lot of different parts, and finally through the eye of the needle. It looked complicated, but their mother could set up a sewing machine almost in her sleep.

At first Alice was doing quite well, but later she seemed to lose her rhythm. The cloth was sticking and she was getting the thread all tangled.

"My fingers are getting sore," she complained.

"Well, then, maybe that's enough for your first time," their mother said.

David and his mother hadn't thought it was strange that Alice's hands had gotten tired, but later that night when they were all in bed Alice began to scream. She was having a nightmare. Their mother ran to her and placed a hand on Alice's forehead.

"Oh, my God! She's burning up with fever!"

CHAPTER 9

David didn't remember very much after that. He recalled his mother telling him to get back to bed. Her voice was calm, but he could see the fear in her eyes. The last thing he could remember for sure was his mother phoning for a doctor.

After that David felt a strange sensation in his chest. It was as if a hand were pressing down on him. The feeling passed quickly. Perhaps it was nothing more than his nerves, but by the next morning he couldn't even lift his head off the pillow. His muscles ached and his body felt weak. Like his sister, he was burning up with fever.

All he wanted to do was sleep. Even to call out to his mother for help seemed like too much effort. He must have eaten sometimes, but he couldn't remember. When he did sleep, the pain and high fever caused terrible nightmares. One night he had a dream that he was falling. Down and down he went, as if he were tumbling down a long flight of stairs.

A week went by before David felt strong enough to sit up on the edge of his bed. But when he did, he realized he didn't know where he was. Although the room was dark, he could tell that it wasn't his bedroom at home. There was a light on nearby and a woman working under it. She was wearing a mask, but David could see she wasn't his mother. He couldn't make sense of it.

"Where am I?" he asked, but the sound barely came out. It sounded like something between a squeak and a croak.

The woman heard him and rushed over with a glass of water. David sipped at it slowly until it eased his scratchy throat.

"Are you hungry?" the woman asked.

David hadn't realized that he was until she said it. He nodded.

"I'll see if I can find you something to eat." She returned a few minutes later carrying a tray with a bowl of soup. Chicken with noodles. The woman put it down on David's lap. "Are you okay with it there?"

David nodded again and started eating. The soup was a little watery, but it was hot and delicious. Hungry as he was, he could only eat slowly. As he did, he glanced around the room. Sheets had been hung up like curtains between the beds, so it was hard to see much. He seemed to be in a small hospital room with a few other beds in it. There were sleeping children in some of them.

"What time is it?" David asked between slurps of soup.

"Almost midnight," the woman told him.

Standing over him, the woman appeared tall and skinny. With her mask on David couldn't see all of her face, but she had light brown hair and blue eyes that seemed kind. "Are you a nurse?" he asked.

"Not really, but I've had some training, so some nights I help out."

"Is this a hospital?"

"Not exactly. You're in the infirmary at the Montefiore Home. We're a Jewish charity."

"But I don't think I'm Jewish."

Her mask shifted slightly as she smiled. "In times like these that's not so important. We've had to take in several new children during the epidemic."

"I caught the flu, didn't I?"

The woman nodded.

"Am I going to die?"

"You're fine now, but you were in pretty rough shape when you came here. It'll still take some time before you get your strength back."

"What about my sister? Is she here, too? Is she all right?"

"Finish your soup," the woman said. "Then I want you to go back to sleep. Someone will talk to you tomorrow."

———

David was still too weak to get out of bed in the morning. An old woman was in the infirmary now, and she brought him a bowl of oatmeal. By lunchtime he was feeling strong enough to get up and walk around a little. Just a few steps, though, and he was exhausted. The old woman helped him get back into bed.

"I'll bring you some soup," she told him. "You need to eat to get your strength back."

It was pea soup this time. Thick and tasty, but a little too salty. When David was done, he asked the woman if he could see his sister.

"The girls are up on the third floor. I don't think you're ready for the stairs yet. Perhaps she's well enough to come down here, though. I'll have to go and see. What's your sister's name?"

"Alice. Alice Saifert."

"Alice Saifert," the woman repeated. "I'll go and find out."

David fell asleep again after the old woman left. When he woke up a while later, the other woman was back again. She was standing at the end of his bed with a man beside her.

"My name is Mrs. Freedman," the woman said. "Do you remember me?"

David nodded. "From last night."

"This is Mr. Rosen. He's here to talk to you."

David sat up slowly. Mrs. Freedman propped an extra pillow behind him so he could sit more comfortably.

"I'm afraid I've got some very bad news for you," Mr. Rosen said.

David didn't understand right away. Then it began to dawn on him. "You mean … Alice …" He couldn't bring himself to say the rest.

Mr. Rosen bobbed his head sadly. "I'm sorry, David. Your sister was just too sick. Nobody could have helped her."

David sat on his bed with a blank look on his face.

"It's all right if you want to cry," Mrs. Freedman said.

David didn't cry. He just stared straight ahead. Then he fixed his eyes on Mr. Rosen. "I want to go home. I want to see my mother." He struggled to his feet. "Where's my mother? I want to see her. I want to go home! I want to see my mother! Someone take me home! Right now!"

He tried to walk toward the door across the room, but there was no way he could make it. Mrs. Freedman put her arms around his shoulders. He was much too weak to put up a struggle as she guided him gently back to his bed.

There was no easy way to say the rest, so Mr. Rosen came straight out with it. "We can't take you home, David. Your mother's dead, too."

This time he couldn't hold back his tears.

CHAPTER 10

It was another two weeks before David was on his feet again. During that time, the war finally ended. The Armistice was announced at 11:00 a.m. on November 11, 1918. The Spanish Flu epidemic seemed to be over, too. It wasn't gone completely, but the worst of it had definitely passed. Once the constant fear was over, it was amazing how quickly people began to forget about it. So many people had lost their lives since the war started in 1914, but the killing and the dying were finished now. People needed to get on with their lives.

David wasn't ready to forget. Not yet. Maybe never. He wanted to know what had happened. How had he gotten to the Montefiore Home?

"It was Abe Salutin," Mrs. Freedman told him.

"Mr. Salutin? From the hat factory?"

"That's right. He was worried when your mother didn't show up for work. She hadn't even called the factory, so he feared the worst. When he tried to telephone your mother, no one answered. So he called the Home. He knew we had volunteers visiting homes, helping to care for people who were sick."

Mrs. Freedman didn't tell David everything. He didn't need to know all the details. It had been a Saturday when he and Alice first got sick. It was Monday afternoon before Mr. Salutin even knew to be worried, and Tuesday before he thought to call the Home. Alice was already dead when the Montefiore volunteers got to their flat on Tuesday afternoon. She was lying in bed with their mother, who was still alive but barely conscious. It was obvious she was very sick. Her lips were already turning blue, and she was wet with sweat from her high fever. She died within an hour. David wasn't in much better shape. His fever was 102 degrees — well above the normal of 98.6. But at least his lungs were clear and he was breathing normally.

"They had to call a fireman to carry you down all those stairs." That was when David had had his dream about falling. "Then they brought you here."

"So what is this place?" David asked, though he was pretty sure he knew the answer already.

"It's an orphanage, David."

He nodded glumly. "My parents were orphans."

"No grandparents then?"

David shook his head.

"Mr. Salutin told us about your father. Are there any other family members we can contact?"

He shook his head again. Tears formed in his eyes.

"It's all right, David," Mrs. Freedman said softly. "You can stay here. I promise you it's not like *Oliver Twist*. The building is new, the beds are comfortable, and the sheets are clean. We'll move you out of the infirmary tonight and into the boys' dormitory. The dining room is downstairs, and there's always enough food to eat. You'll need to eat to get your strength back, David. You're awfully skinny right now. Do you know what you weighed before you got sick?"

David shook his head.

"How old are you?" she asked.

"I'm thirteen. Almost fourteen."

"You're a little on the small side for your age, but a boy like you should weigh close to a hundred pounds ..."

Mrs. Freedman led David over to a scale. He stepped on, and she slid the weights around until they balanced.

"Hmm," she said. "Only eighty-two pounds. We're going to have to do something about that. Are you ready for lunch?"

"Can I eat up here?" David asked. He wasn't ready to meet anyone new yet and have to talk about what happened.

Mrs. Freedman understood. "I'll take you downstairs, but you don't have to eat in the dining room if you don't want to. J-P can bring you your lunch in the pantry."

The only way to get down from the second floor was

on a staircase outside the building. Mrs. Freedman led David down. He looked around at the children eating at the long tables. There were quite a few. "We're full up," Mrs. Freedman said. "Sixty-five children. The oldest are sixteen. The youngest are six. We don't have any babies here."

Mrs. Freedman took David through the dining room and into the pantry. It was a small, closed room right next to the kitchen. The people who worked in the kitchen used the pantry for storing cans and other dry food, as well as some of the kitchen utensils. There was also a small table with a few chairs around it, where the kitchen staff usually ate their meals.

"Will you be all right if I leave you alone?" Mrs. Freedman asked.

David shrugged and crooked his head a bit.

"I'll tell J-P you're here. Come back to the infirmary when you're done and we'll find someone to take you to the dormitory."

David wasn't sure if J-P was a name or the initials for some kind of job. He was trying to think what it might stand for when a young man limped in. He had thick black hair parted in the middle and a face that was a little pudgy, though the rest of him seemed wiry and strong. David guessed he was about twenty-five and had probably been wounded during the war. He was also missing the last two fingers on his left hand. David tried not to stare.

"Brought you a sandwich," J-P said. "Bring you anodder if you want. They say we're supposed to fatten you up."

"You're French," David said. "I didn't know any Jews were French."

J-P laughed. "I'm not Jewish. I just work here. Help out in da kitchen and be Shabbas Goy on Saturdays."

David didn't know that expression. His face must have shown it.

"Saturday's da Jewish Sunday," J-P explained. "And religious Jews aren't supposed to work on da Sabbath. From sundown Friday to sundown on Saturday, they don't even turn on a light or use da stove. People here aren't like that so much, but a lotta people who give them money are. So they gotta stick by da rules. But da rules say someone who's not Jewish can do those things, so that's me."

David ate his sandwich as J-P explained. It was some sort of dry roast beef with spicy mustard.

"Brisket," J-P said. "It's good, eh?"

David nodded.

"You want more?"

"Yes, please. And some milk, too?"

J-P went out and got him another sandwich. He also brought him a glass of grape juice. "You can't have milk with meat," he said. "It's not kosher."

J-P sat with David while he ate. "J-P's your name?" David asked between bites.

"Da English people, they say J-P because they can't pronounce it. It's really Jean-Patrice. Jean-Patrice de la Montagne," he said with a fancy bow. "John Patrick of da Mountain."

David laughed. "I'm just David. David Saifert."

"You're one of da ones they brought here with da *grippe*, right?"

David mumbled "Yes" as he ate.

"You going home now that you're better?" David looked down, and J-P realized he'd made a mistake. "Sorry, kid. I didn't know ..."

David just nodded.

"There's pudding for dessert. I'll get you some ..."

When David finished eating, he went back upstairs.

"I'd like to go home," he told Mrs. Freedman.

"But, David ..." She looked alarmed. "I thought you understood."

"I know. I do. I just want to see it. That's all."

David couldn't really put what he was feeling into words, but his mother and sister had both been buried while he was still sick. Like his father's death, it was hard to feel these were real. He didn't want to go to the cemetery to see where they were, but he had to go someplace where he could say some sort of goodbye. Going home seemed like the best place to do that.

"Of course," Mrs. Freedman said. "I'll see what I can do."

About an hour later Mr. Rosen was driving David home. It was the first time he'd ever been in a car. It was big and black, with spoke wheels like fat bicycle tires and two glass headlamps in front that reminded him of googly eyes. The ride was smoother than in a streetcar, but the car jerked every time it stopped and started. David remembered what his father had said about horses and cars on the way home from their first hockey game. Mr. Rosen's car was a little noisy, but at least it didn't poop!

It was only about a fifteen-minute drive from the Montefiore Home to Chabot Street. Arriving by car somehow made the street seem smaller than David had ever realized. All the buildings were so tightly packed. Mr. Rosen parked the car in front and rang the bell for the first-floor flat. Mr. Lemoine, the landlord, came to the door. Mr. Rosen had telephoned ahead, so Mr. Lemoine was expecting them. David had never spoken to him much, but his parents had lived in the flat for a long time and they'd been good tenants. Even when times were tough, they always paid their bills.

Mr. Lemoine wasn't sure what to say. He just grimaced at David, who was carrying a small box they had given him at the Home to collect some of his things. "Your mother was a real nice lady," he said. Then he led David and Mr. Rosen up the stairs. "It'll be cold inside," he told them as they climbed. He had opened all the windows so the flat could air out. "And I burned all the clothes," he whispered to Mr. Rosen. "The sheets and blankets, too."

"Probably wise," Mr. Rosen said. "We've already arranged for new clothes to be donated for the boy."

When they got to the top, Mr. Lemoine unlocked the door. It was obvious he had no intention of coming inside. "Just leave it when you're done. I'll lock up later." Then he turned and went back down.

Mr. Rosen held open the door for David, and they went inside. It was cold. Somehow it was even colder inside than it had been on the stairs. David could almost see his father putting a couple of logs into the heater. There were still dishes in the drying rack beside the sink in the kitchen, and a bad smell came from the icebox. Mr. Lemoine hadn't thought to empty it. Despite the cold in the flat, all the ice had melted long ago. No one had been there to empty the pan, and there was water all over the floor. It made David feel even too sad to cry. He turned away and went to his room.

David picked up his scrapbooks and put them in the box. He took down some of the pictures from the wall and placed them in the box, as well. He'd heard Mr. Lemoine and Mr. Rosen talking about the clothes. He knew his dresser drawers would be empty, but he opened them, anyway. In the bottom drawer he saw his sewing kit. David stared at it for a moment, then took it out. He unfastened the snap and opened the leather sides. Inside were several needles of varying lengths and thicknesses, plus a few safety pins. There were three cardboard spools of thread, a collection of buttons, a thimble to protect his thumb, and a small pair of scissors for cutting thread.

He closed the kit and put it back in the drawer. Then, as he pushed the drawer shut, he changed his mind. It didn't feel right to leave the kit behind, as if it would disappoint his mother if he did. So he put it in the box, too.

David went into his parents' room next. He stared at the bed for a long time. It was just a grey mattress on a metal frame, but it reminded David of a skeleton, which seemed about right. On top of the dresser was a carrying case where his mother kept her thread. He opened it and threw some of the spools into his box. The family had very few photographs, but there were some on the far wall in this bedroom. David walked over and studied them. There was one of his mother and father, and another of David and Alice. There was also one of the four of them together. They had been taken early in the summer of 1916, before his father had joined the army. Everyone looked a lot younger.

Mr. Rosen had been silent as David strode through the house, but he spoke now. "You should take them," he said of the photographs. "It's painful now, but one day you'll be glad you have them."

David felt as if that would never be true, but then he remembered something. "Uncle Danny!" He rushed back to the dresser and pulled opened the top drawer. Nothing was in there. No stack of letters. No folder with the half-photo.

He spun around angrily. Mr. Lemoine must have burned them with the clothes. But then David spotted the folder. It was sitting on the small wooden table next to the bed. There was a pencil there, too. David could see that something had been written on the folder. It was faint, as if it had been scribbled by someone too weak to press down properly. The printing was sloppy, but David recognized it as his mother's. She had written two words on the folder protecting her brother's picture: *Find him.*

CHAPTER 11

David couldn't wait to show the picture to Mrs. Freedman when he got back to the Home.

"This is my Uncle Danny," he said. "I could live with him!"

Mrs. Freedman saw what was written on the folder and opened it. She was surprised when she saw the picture. Not just because the face looked so much like David's, but because the boy in the picture was even younger than David was.

"When was this taken?" she asked.

"I don't know exactly," David said. "A long time ago, I guess. My mother said he was ten or eleven."

"He's your mother's brother?"

"Yes."

"And there's no picture of what he looks like now?"

"No."

"But he's the only relative you're aware of?"

"Yes." David was getting impatient.

Mrs. Freedman picked up a pencil and paper. "Do you know his last name?"

David tried to remember. His mother usually just called him Danny. "Embury!" he said suddenly. "Danny Embury."

"And he lives in Montreal?"

"No. He lives in Seattle."

Mrs. Freedman's brow wrinkled briefly. "Seattle, Washington?"

"I guess so. Out west. Near Vancouver."

She nodded. "Do you know his address?"

"No ..."

Mrs. Freedman did her very best to keep the doubt out of her voice. "Well, David, we can try. But it won't be easy."

David moved into the boys' dormitory that night. It was a large L-shaped room with a wooden floor and small windows on the outside wall. There were about a dozen beds in one part of the L, with eight lined up under the windows against the long part of the wall, and four across from them. There were about the same number of beds inside the other part of the L. There were lockers, like in school, along the two ends of the dorm where the boys kept their clothes. David put the box with his scrapbooks and pictures beneath his bed. It was a nice bed, not a cot, with a thick mattress. When no one was looking, David tucked his sewing kit under the foot of his mattress. He didn't know what people here would make of it, but he didn't want it to be among the first things these boys knew about him.

The children in the Home were divided into three groups. Group One included the children who were six to nine. They were called Group One because they were the first to go to bed at night. Group Two were aged ten to thirteen, and Group Three were the children between fourteen and sixteen. David was in Group Two. An older boy named Meyer from Group Three showed him around.

"Mostly things are pretty good here," Meyer told him. "We watch out for each other. But there are always a couple of troublemakers. There's a boy named Benny in your group who's always looking for a fight."

The boys took turns sweeping the floor in the dorm, and the first time Meyer told Benny to take the broom and sweep, Benny shoved him and said, "Make me!"

"Watch out for Solly in my group, too. He's always getting his mouth washed out with soap for swearing. If you hang around him, you will, too. But he's not really a troublemaker. More of a kibbitzer, really."

David didn't understand that word.

"A kibbitzer's a joker," Meyer explained. "Solly likes to fool around. I forgot that you're not Jewish."

"My father was Jewish."

"Doesn't count. Your mother's the one who has to be Jewish."

"She's not," said David, who wasn't used yet to saying *wasn't* when he was talking about his mother.

"Then you're not."

Meyer didn't say that in a mean way. Still, David wasn't sure where he stood as a non-Jew in a Jewish orphanage. "We never went to church or anything," he said.

"Well, now I guess you'll be going to *shul*," Meyer said.

"*Shul?*"

"Synagogue. We have services in the auditorium every Saturday morning. They'll make you go. Everyone has to. Don't know if they'll bother sending you to the Hebrew school, though."

David discovered that the Home ran its own Hebrew school. It also had a library with books in English and a reading room where kids could study or do their homework. They all went to a regular day school a couple of blocks away.

Schools and other public places had opened again while David was recovering. Still, the people at the Home thought David wasn't strong enough for full days at school. It was already near the end of November, so they decided he could wait to begin school after the break for Christmas and New Year's.

The Home was nearly empty when everyone else went to school. Of course, there was always some of the staff around. Sometimes David helped Mrs. Freedman in the office. That was where she usually worked when there were no emergencies in the infirmary. He did things for her like filing papers or stamping envelopes. A few were addressed to charities and other Jewish groups in Seattle.

"I hope someone there will be able to find out something for us," she told him.

During the week, David worked with the kitchen staff to set the tables for when the other kids came home for lunch. Often he helped J-P stock the shelves in the pantry, too. Although David was supposed to get to know the other kids in the Home, he often ate his lunch with J-P in the pantry.

J-P usually had a French newspaper with him. David couldn't understand many of the words, but he did recognize some of the names and pictures, especially as the hockey season neared.

"That's Newsy Lalonde," David said over J-P's shoulder one day in early December. "What's the story say?"

"Da Canadiens are starting practice this week. Lalonde's been working out in a gym da past couple of weeks and they say he's already in great shape. With the war over a lot more players will be back in da game. Dey're calling it the Peace Season. You a hockey fan?"

"Yeah," David said. "My father used to take me to games."

"Wanderers, eh?"

"No, the Canadiens. He said he liked the way they played."

"Smart man, your father."

David was quiet.

J-P didn't say anything for a while, either. Then he asked, "What happened to him?"

"I don't really know. We got a telegram, but it didn't say much."

J-P nodded. "It was pretty bad over there. I lost my bruder at Passchendaele. One minute Jacques was standing beside me, next minute *boom* and he was gone. They told me dere was nothing left but his boots. Blast knocked me out for three days, but all I lost was a couple of fingers and some muscle in my thigh. Couldn't march after that, though. They had to send me home."

That was the most David had ever heard a soldier talk about the war. Most of them didn't like to speak of it except to other soldiers. No one else could really understand.

David brought their conversation back to hockey. "First game I went to, Joe Hall pushed Newsy into the boards and he got cut for ten stitches."

"I was dere, too! That Hall's a ... well, I don't wanna say around here what he is, but I can't believe dey're teammates now."

"I know, but they got along so well last season they even roomed together on road trips. There were lots of stories about it."

It surprised a lot of people how well Hall and Newsy got along as teammates, but the Bad Man of hockey still had his temper. At a game in Toronto during the season Hall got into a stick-swinging duel with one of their players. It was so bad that the police charged them after the game and they had to go to court.

"Boy, my bruder hated that guy! Jacques always said he'd love to get Bad Joe into da ring and show him a thing or two." J-P smiled at the memory. "My bruder was a wrestler. He was a lot bigger than me and used to fight on da cards Mr. Kennedy promoted at da Athletic Club before da war.

"Even though Mr. Kennedy was running da Canadiens, too, Jacques and I always sneaked into da Arena to see them play. Dere was a window above da maintenance room that was almost always open. Usually, we'd have to wait till da end of da first period when da workers were shovelling snow off da ice. Jacques boosted me up to have a look. If dere wasn't anyone inside, I'd climb in and open da door for him. Then we'd blend into the standing room section and watch da last two periods free!"

J-P glanced over at David, and a sly smile spread across his lips. "You're kind of small, aren't you? If dere's a window like that at da Jubilee, I bet I could boost you up to it."

CHAPTER 12

The new hockey season was scheduled to start on Saturday night, December 21, 1918. The Canadiens would be at home to the Ottawa Senators. J-P hadn't said anything more about trying to sneak into games, but as the season approached, there were certainly more and more hockey stories to read in the newspapers.

"They've introduced some new rules this season," J-P told David after reading about them in one of his French newspapers. "From now on when a player gets a penalty his team won't be able to replace him with someone else. They'll have to play a man short till da penalty's over."

David nodded. "Makes sense." It really hadn't hurt the team much before when a player got a penalty. Now the other team would get a real advantage. "What's the other rule?"

"Forward passing," J-P said. "Dey're finally gonna allow it. Dey're gonna paint two blue lines on da ice twenty feet eider side of centre. When you're inside da lines, you can pass da puck forward to any other player inside the lines, too. They say it'll speed up da game."

Both new rules had already been used out west in the Pacific Coast Hockey Association. The PCHA was a rival league with teams in British Columbia and the western United States. For several years their champion had been meeting the NHA or NHL champion after the season to battle for the Stanley Cup. The series was played in the east one year, and out west the next. Throughout the war years, people had wondered if the two leagues should have kept on playing. Attendance everywhere had fallen way off. Both the NHL and the PCHA had been reduced to three teams each, but now that the war was over it seemed as if everyone was a hockey fan again. J-P's newspaper made that very clear on the day of the game between the Canadiens and Ottawa: CE SOIR, L'OUVERTURE DU HOCKEY PROFESSIONEL À MONTRÉAL.

The headline was written in French, so J-P translated for David: TONIGHT, THE OPENING OF PROFESSIONAL HOCKEY IN MONTREAL. David could probably have figured that out, but the language in the rest of the article was much too difficult for him.

"It says," J-P told David, "that fans have been waiting for da game feverishly because this is da first time in four years they can take pleasure at a hockey game with no worries or unhappiness. It says in da past da war put heavy conditions on sports, and no one was sure of da future. But now sports are normal again."

J-P read on a bit more before translating. "Basically, it says that sports are getting back to normal all over da world and Canada can't lag behind. It says da boom in sports is real and must be felt in every soul."

The French newspaper made it sound as if it was everyone's duty to cheer for the Canadiens. But it wasn't so easy to follow the team. Only about three thousand fans could jam into Jubilee Rink, and if you weren't at the game, it was pretty hard to find out what happened. For big games out of town, newspapers often made arrangements to provide fans with special bulletins. People could wait outside a newspaper office and hear reports read off the telegraph wires. Sometimes they even reserved hotel ballrooms or theatres so that people could wait inside to get the reports. But it was rare that anyone went to those extremes for home games. Now that telephones were more popular, you could call the newspaper and ask for the score. David had never done that before, and he certainly wasn't going to be able to do it from the Home. For one thing, the office with the telephone was closed well before games ended around ten o'clock at night. And even if it wasn't, lights out for David's group was earlier than that, anyway.

So David went to bed on Saturday night with no idea how the Canadiens had done against the Senators. Although word around the Home the next morning was that the Habs had lost, none of the major Montreal newspapers printed a Sunday edition, so David still didn't have any details about the game until Monday.

School was closed now for the Christmas break, and the Home didn't empty out as usual after breakfast. David hadn't really made any friends among the other orphans yet, so he was still happy to spend time helping J-P in the pantry, especially since he knew J-P would have a newspaper handy. In fact, the newspaper was lying on the table in the pantry, open to the sports news on page six, when David got there. He saw the headline right away: LE CANADIEN PERD SAMEDI. MANQUANT DE FORME ET JOUANT SUR UNE GLACE MOLLE ET PESANTE, L'ÉQUIPE EST BATTUE PAR LES OTTAWA PAR 5–2.

He knew what some of it meant. The Canadiens had lost on Saturday. He also recognized that the score was 5–2. But that was about it.

"What does it say?" David asked.

J-P translated. "'Out of shape and on soft, heavy ice, da team was beaten by Ottawa.' Da whole story pretty much goes on like that. It says da team isn't in proper condition yet and that they would've won if they were in better shape. Still, it says it was an exciting game — 'one of da best in Montreal in many years.' It was only 3–2 Ottawa until da last few minutes, but da Canadiens ran out of steam at da end."

David picked up the paper and glanced at the summary. The Canadiens had scored first one minute into the game, but Ottawa had tied it a few seconds later. It was 2–1 Ottawa after one and 3–1 early in the second period before Newsy Lalonde cut the lead to 3–2.

"Da newspaper says Newsy played well," J-P told him. "He proved he's still da team's star. Vézina was good, too. He faced a lot of shots and didn't have a chance on most of da goals."

David spotted the cartoon of Georges Vézina beside the story. It showed him standing tall, towering over the net behind him. *"Le Roi des goalers,"* the caption read.

"King of da Goalies," J-P translated.

Another cartoon revealed a Canadiens player being flattened by a large weight with Ottawa and the number five written on it. There was also an illustration depicting Ottawa's goalie and defencemen putting up a brick wall across their end of the ice.

"They play again in Toronto tonight," J-P said. "Hopefully, they'll do better."

And they did. In the newspaper on Tuesday, David and J-P learned all about the Canadiens' 4–3 win over the Arenas. The Toronto team seemed to have the game in hand with a 3–1 lead after two periods, but the Canadiens rallied for three goals in the third. Newsy Lalonde got the winner with only a couple of minutes left. *"Lalonde et Vézina ont brillé,"* the words beneath the headline said.

"They were brilliant?" David asked.

"They 'shined,' actually," J-P said. "But I guess it's really da same thing." Then he smiled. "You know, my sister, Marie, and her husband live out near da Jubilee. I'm going to spend Christmas with them. I figure I'll take a walk by da rink while I'm dere. The Canadiens are back home against Toronto on Saturday. If I like what I see, I think we should go to that game."

———

Being a Jewish orphanage, the Montefiore Home didn't celebrate Christmas. David was glad not to have to think about it. His family had never made a big fuss over holidays, but his mother always cooked a special meal for Christmas, and there were usually a few presents. Mostly, it was something practical like new boots for the winter. Still, it would have been hard to celebrate his first Christmas in an orphanage so soon after losing his family. The fact that the Home didn't do anything for Hanukkah, either, made it even easier to act as if there wasn't any Christmas at all.

Really, the only thing that was any different than normal around the Home was that J-P was away for a couple of days. While he was gone, David wondered what he would find at Jubilee Rink. Would there be a window J-P could boost him up to? The thought of sneaking in to see a game was pretty exciting, but it made David a little nervous, as well. What would happen if they got caught?

"Don't worry about that," J-P told David when he got back on Friday morning. "They'll just kick us out if they catch us. It's not like they send you to jail or anything."

"So we're going?"

"We're going!"

J-P had to make special arrangements to take David out of the Home on Saturday evening. With the sun setting so early in December, the Jewish Sabbath was officially over a little after five o'clock, so that was no problem. J-P and David could leave the Home any time after supper. However, the hockey game wouldn't end until about ten o'clock. It would take at least forty-five minutes to get back to the Home on the streetcar and that would make it well after lights out. None of the children were allowed in or out of the Home after bedtime. So David and J-P were going to spend the night at his sister's house. David had to pack a small bag with some overnight things.

"We'll drop off your things at Marie's first, so you won't have to carry them with you to da game," J-P explained. "Da game starts at 8:15, so da first period will end around a quarter to nine. It's about a fifteen-minute walk from my sister's house, so if we leave dere by 8:30 we'll be fine. We should leave here by 7:15, so we have plenty of time."

The weather was nice for late December, but it would get cold during their long evening, so David was bundled up in his warmest clothes when he met J-P in front of the Home. They made the short trip down Jeanne-Mance Street to Mount Royal Avenue. A streetcar ran across Mount Royal, but it was only four blocks along the avenue, across Saint Urbain, to Saint Lawrence Boulevard, so they walked to catch the streetcar there. When it arrived, David looked for the trolley car number just as he'd always done when he was a little boy. It was number 129. He and J-P got on and rode the streetcar all the way into the heart of downtown. They got off at Saint Catherine Street and waited for the streetcar that would take them out to the east end.

Streetcars from several different routes used the long stretch of Saint Catherine. "Which one do we want?" David asked.

"Whichever comes first," J-P told him. "Any one of them will get us out dere. Da streetcar offices are a couple of blocks from da Jubilee."

After a few minutes, the 3A streetcar screeched to a stop. David spotted the number 767 as they got on.

The ride along Saint Catherine out to Jubilee Rink was nearly twice as long as the journey into downtown. As they got farther from the Home, David felt safe to ask J-P something he'd been wondering about. "What happens to the kids in the orphanage after they turn sixteen?"

"They have to go. It's da rule."

David remembered that his mother had left the orphanage she grew up in to work in the rooming house when she was sixteen. "But how do they know where they can go?"

"How old are you?" J-P asked.

"I'm thirteen. I'll be fourteen pretty soon, though."

"So you're in grade eight?"

David nodded.

"Most kids at da Home get jobs after they turn fourteen," J-P told him. "It costs money for high school, and most don't have any, so they start working after grade eight. Da Home makes it so when dey're sixteen they'll have a few dollars saved up. That way, if they've got family, they can move in with them and earn their keep. Otherwise someone from da Home helps them find a place to live."

"Like in a rooming house?"

"Yeah."

"But what if you can't get a job and you don't have a family?"

"Well, they don't kick you outta da orphanage right away, but I suppose a kid like that might end up on a farm in the Eastern Townships."

David nodded. "My father was on a farm there when he came to Canada. He once told me they worked him like a slave."

"That's what I heard, too. You get a place to live and enough food, but they don't pay much and they work you really hard. I know a lot of people who joined da army to get away from da farms. So what about you? Do you have udder family in Montreal?"

David shook his head. "My mother has a brother, but he lives in Seattle. I showed Mrs. Freedman a picture. She sent some letters to try to find him."

"You don't know where he is?"

"Uh-uh. My mother hadn't seen him since he was a boy."

J-P frowned. "You probably don't want to hear this, but every orphan dreams about things like that. They all think they've got a long-lost cousin or a rich uncle some-where who's going to show up one day and save them."

"But I do have an uncle!" David insisted. "And I'm going to find him!"

J-P heard the angry tone in David's voice and regretted what he'd said. He knew it was true, but it was stupid of him to say it. David had lost so much so recently. There was no reason to take his hope away, too. And it wasn't impossible that if he did have an uncle that someone would find him. It was a real long shot, though.

"I'm sure Mrs. Freedman will do all she can," J-P said reassuringly. "She's a real nice lady. Besides, you still got two more years."

Two more years!

David hoped it wouldn't take that long. He knew his mother had done it when she was only sixteen, but David couldn't imagine himself living alone in a rooming house. He had to find his uncle.

CHAPTER 13

The trip on the streetcar along Saint Catherine from downtown to Jubilee Rink was pretty much the same as the one David used to take along Dorchester with his parents to get home from the hat factory. It was dark, and there wasn't really much to see, but David could pretty much tell when the streetcar was getting close to Papineau Avenue. That was where they used to transfer to head for their flat on Chabot.

A few minutes after they crossed the intersection at Papineau, J-P and David got off the streetcar at Frontenac Street. J-P's sister lived a few blocks away on La Fontaine. It only took about five minutes to walk there.

J-P's sister and her husband had a small house in a working-class neighbourhood. The streets in this area didn't look too different from streets around Chabot, but practically everyone here in the east end of Montreal was French. Marie didn't even speak English. When they went inside, she said something to J-P that made him laugh.

"She say you don't look Jewish," he translated.

David was quiet as everyone sat together in the kitchen and J-P spoke with his sister and brother-in-law. He noticed that they both called him Jean-Patrice, but otherwise they spoke so fast that David couldn't make out the words. Judging from the smiles and laughter, he could at least tell they were happy. Marie brought out some treats for all of them, and some mugs of hot coffee for J-P and her husband, Maurice. Maurice opened a small brown bottle and poured something alcoholic into their coffee.

"Ah, merci," J-P said.

That was finally a word David recognized. *"Mair-see,"* he said to J-P's sister as he picked up a piece of pastry.

"De rien," she replied with a smile.

After a few minutes, J-P told David it was time to go. They bundled up again into their warm winter wear and headed out once more into the cold night.

"Do they know what we're doing?" David asked J-P as they walked.

"Well, I told them we were going to da game ..."

"But do they know what we're *doing*?" David asked again.

J-P laughed. "Well, me and Jacques never used to say anything to Marie about sneaking into da Arena, but I'm sure Maurice knows da game started at 8:15 and it's already 8:30!"

The stretch along Saint Catherine beyond Frontenac

was mostly open railway land. The wind whipped in off the Saint Lawrence River and blew freezing cold across the open spaces. Fortunately, it only took a few more minutes to reach Jubilee Rink.

David knew from all the newspaper stories at the time of the fire that Jubilee Rink was much smaller than Westmount Arena. Still, he was surprised when they reached the building. The Arena had been two storeys of red brick with fancy concrete finishings along the line of the roof. And while it was true the Arena looked like a factory from the outside, Jubilee Rink was nothing more than a wooden barn. And the walls were pretty thin, too, so it would stay cold inside and keep the ice frozen. Only the sounds coming from inside really made it clear what the building was. It was easy to hear the fans cheering while David and J-P stood in the street.

"Hope that means dey're finishing up da first period and not already starting da second," J-P said. "It's way too cold to wait here much longer." Fortunately, the noise died down a few minutes later. "It must be intermission now. Let's go."

He led David around to the back of the building. As they walked, David could see that most of the windows were too high for anyone to reach without a ladder, but a few were low enough.

"This is it," J-P said, pointing at a narrow window beyond a wooden door. The window, which swung on a hinge from the side, was a little too high to see through, but David noticed it was open a crack. "First thing we gotta do is make sure da room's empty. If I get down on my hands and knees, you can stand on my back and see in."

"Are you sure?"

"Just don't stand dere too long!"

David stepped onto J-P's back and peered in the window. He spied a workbench with a bunch of drawers against one wall and a lot of big tools scattered around. There was also a potbellied stove to keep the room warm, but no people. "There's no one inside," he said, jumping down.

"Okay," J-P said. "Here's what you gotta do now. Climb on my back again and reach your hand inside. The window should pull open pretty easy. Then I'll boost you up. Once you're inside, open da door for me."

The hinge on the window was a little bit stiffer than J-P had described, but it pulled open without too much trouble. When it was open, J-P got up and linked his hands like a stirrup for a horse to boost David up. Once he got his knee onto the windowsill, it was pretty easy to get inside. His heart was pounding from the excitement and the exercise, and David had to take a few deep breaths to calm himself. But then there was a problem.

"The door's locked," David whispered out the window.

"Can't you find da latch or something?"

"No, there's a big piece of wood across it, and it's held in place with a padlock."

David heard J-P mutter some words that would have gotten his mouth washed out with soap if he were a kid at the orphanage. Then he said, "I'll have to come in through da window then."

"But it's too high for you to reach."

"Maybe dere's something you can throw down for me?"

David looked around quickly and spotted the perfect thing — a stepladder about three feet long. He lowered it out the window, and J-P climbed up effortlessly. The ladder was even tall enough that J-P could reach out the window and haul it back inside. But when he did he caught the sleeve of his coat on something sharp on the metal frame around the window and tore a long rip in the fabric.

"I can fix that for you," David said without thinking.

J-P wasn't really listening, though. He just glanced at his sleeve, then ignored it. "Come on. Let's get outta here before da workmen get back."

From the inside, Jubilee Rink seemed a lot more like Westmount Arena, but on a much smaller scale. The ice was the same size, but where Westmount Arena had twelve rows of seats, Jubilee had five. In some places there were just three. And it only had seats on the long sides of the rink. There was nothing but standing room at the two ends. Up in the rafters, large globe-shaped bulbs hung down to light the playing surface. There were also flags of all different sizes, shapes, and colours suspended from the metal beams that supported the wooden roof.

David and J-P made their way to the far side of the rink from the maintenance room and blended into the crowd standing behind the net at that end.

"C'est quoi le score?" J-P asked the man standing next to him.

"Un-zero Canadiens," he said.

"Qui a marqué?"

"Lalonde," the man said, *"un but de tout beauté."*

After that the French words were too fast for David to follow. J-P filled him in when the man was done.

"With da weather so cold, he say da ice is much faster tonight." Jubilee Rink had natural ice, so the weather could make a big difference. "Da Canadiens came out flying from da start. They kept Toronto bottled up in their own end, but they couldn't score. About halfway through da period, Lalonde rushed da puck from end to end for a beautiful goal. After that Toronto came on strong, but Vézina was too good for them."

Just then the two teams returned to the ice and lined up to start the second period. Toronto would be coming their way this period. Georges Vézina was in the goal right in front of them.

"I see he's still wearing his toque," J-P said.

Vézina always wore a toque in the Canadiens' colours of red, white, and blue. When he joined Montreal in 1910, the rules said goalies had to remain standing all the time. They weren't allowed to fall on the ice to make saves. Those rules had changed, but Vézina still rarely left his feet. He played with an extra-long stick and used it to knock down as many pucks as he ever caught in his glove, and he always seemed so cool and calm while guarding his net that he often appeared bored by it all. Playing goal was tough, but nobody ever heard Vézina complain. In fact, they rarely heard him speak at all. In French, people called him *l'Habitant silencieux*.

The Canadiens had Joe Malone at centre to start the second period and dropped Lalonde back to play defence with Joe Hall. Malone won the faceoff, pushing the puck ahead of him and then rushing it into the Toronto end. The Canadiens put the pressure on quickly, but they couldn't fire the puck into the net. From where David and J-P stood, it was a long way down to the other side, but they had a pretty good view soon enough. Unfortunately, it wasn't what they wanted to see. Toronto defenceman Harry Cameron went end to end and beat Vézina for a goal. Just one minute in, the score was tied 1–1.

The crowd groaned and was still grumbling as the teams lined up for another faceoff. Malone won it again, but this time he drew the puck back to his former Quebec teammate, Joe Hall.

J-P shook his head, seeing the Bad Man in the red, white, and blue *tricolore* of the Canadiens. He muttered something in French. David didn't know what his friend had said, but he imagined it was something like "I can't believe it."

Hall was still as tough as ever, but he was one of the good guys now. He skated quickly across the blue line and fired a forward pass to Didier Pitre. At five feet eleven inches and 185 pounds, Pitre was one of the biggest men in hockey. French newspapers now called him *le 75 de la NHL* after the powerful seventy-five-millimetre field guns from France that so many armies had used in the war. The husky right winger was the player picked on the most for being out of shape in the opening game. He seemed determined to make up for that in this one. Pitre launched a booming shot from just across centre ice. His Cannonball blast put the Canadiens back on top less than ten seconds after Toronto had tied it! The fans cheered while his teammates mussed his hair.

Shortly after the next faceoff, Odie Cleghorn sprang Lalonde free with a forward pass. He didn't shoot from centre but carried the puck all the way into the Toronto end. It was now 3–1 Canadiens, and the second period wasn't even two minutes old.

The speed slowed down after that, but Pitre kept going at a furious pace.

"Nothing wrong with him tonight," J-P said.

Shortly before the period ended, Pitre scored again and the Canadiens took a three-goal lead into the intermission.

"It's a good rule change, da forward pass," J-P said. "It really speeds things up."

David agreed. "I hope they score as many goals when they're coming into our end this period."

During the break in play, three workmen came out onto the ice to shovel off the snow. David watched them nervously at first, thinking they might somehow spot him in the crowd and know what he'd done.

J-P noticed the tense look on David's face and smiled. "Don't worry. If dey're thinking anything, it's only 'I thought I left that ladder over dere.'"

The Canadiens came out fast again to start the third period. Just two minutes in, Malone set up Cleghorn for a goal. Toronto got that one back quickly, but then Hall scored three minutes later. Toronto got another

one late in the period, but then with two minutes to go
a Toronto defenceman slashed Cleghorn. He was sent to
the penalty box, and Toronto had to finish the game one
player short. The Canadiens didn't score with their man
advantage, but they still wound up with a 6–3 victory.

The crowd was excited as the people spilled onto Saint
Catherine Street. There were lots of people strolling back
to their homes around the neighbourhood while David
and J-P made their way back to his sister's. It was only
a little after ten when they returned to the house, but
Marie and Maurice were already in bed. J-P explained
that they'd be up early in the morning to go to church.

Marie had made up a bed in the spare room and had
left some blankets on a sofa in the parlour. "You take da
bedroom," J-P said. "I'll sleep out here."

It had been an exciting evening, and it took David
quite a while to fall asleep. Some time later, in the middle
night, he was awakened by a terrible sound.

David's eyes shot open. At first he had no idea
where he was. Then he remembered. But everything
was suddenly so silent that he wondered if he'd really
heard anything. Then it came again — a high-pitched
scream from the front of the house. Then someone was
shouting. It was J-P.

"Jacques! Jacques! Que s'est-il passé? Où est mon frère?"
Then there was another scream.

David heard Marie rush out of her room. She woke her brother and was able to calm him down. He was silent for the rest of the night, but David had a hard time getting back to sleep.

———

David would never have said anything about it, but J-P brought up his nightmare toward the end of their long streetcar ride back to the Home on Sunday morning.

"Sometimes I have bad dreams about da war. Hope I didn't scare you or anything."

He had, but David didn't think it would be right to say so. "Sometimes I have dreams about my family, too."

David's dreams weren't really nightmares, but they were always sad. At first it seemed as if everything was okay, but then something always happened in the dream to make David realize his family had all died and he was alone.

"It was fun last night, though, wasn't it?" J-P asked.

"Yeah. It was a great game."

"But I'll have to ask Mrs. Wolfe to fix my coat." J-P held up his arm to show the damaged sleeve.

In all the excitement of the evening, David had forgotten about the rip in J-P's coat. "I can fix that for you."

"Yeah?" J-P didn't look as if he believed it.

"I can ... if you want me to."

When they got back to the Home, David went up to the boys' dormitory and carefully got the sewing kit out from under his mattress. He took it down to meet J-P in the pantry. He also brought the picture of his Uncle Danny to show him.

"Boy, same eyes," J-P said. "Same hair. He look just like you."

"I know."

"What's his name?"

"Danny. Danny Embury."

"Probably goes by Daniel now," J-P said. "Or maybe just Dan. So how come it's cut in half like that?"

David told J-P the story his mother had told him. "It was the only picture of my mother and her brother together. When the family that adopted him moved away, they cut it in half and both of them kept the part with the other one in it."

J-P kept staring at the photo, then glanced at David and shook his head. "It's almost spooky."

While J-P studied the photo, David thought about the words his mother had written on the folder. *Find him*.

"I wish I could just go to Seattle myself," David said. He knew it sounded too silly to say out loud, but he believed their strong resemblance would bring them together somehow if he could only get close enough to where his uncle was.

J-P shook his head. "It's a long way to go on your own. I don't know how you could do it."

"Neither do I," David admitted.

Seattle was three thousand miles away, and it was in a different country. It would take a week to ride a train from Montreal to Vancouver, and it would cost about $60 for the cheapest ticket. That was a full month's salary for many working people. And that wouldn't even pay for a mattress and a pillow to sleep on the train, or for any food along the way. Then it would cost more money to get from Vancouver to Seattle. He couldn't just sleep on the street when he got there, either. He'd have to pay for somewhere to stay. And who could know how long it would take? Besides, what would he actually do if he got there? Wander the streets looking for a grown man who looked like him?

It all seemed impossible. And probably crazy. It was best not even to think about it too much and hope that the letters Mrs. Freedman was sending would eventually find his uncle.

"So can you really fix this?" J-P asked, tossing his coat onto the table. "It's a pretty big rip."

David knew he could do it easily, but he was a little surprised how much he actually wanted to. It only took him a few minutes, and J-P's coat looked as good as new.

"Lemme see that," J-P said, picking up his coat and giving the sleeve a good going over. He ran his fingers along where the tear used to be. "Real smooth. You can barely tell it was ripped. How'd you learn to sew like that?"

"My mother taught me." David didn't go into any of the details. "I used to help her."

"You're really good," J-P said. "You shouldn't be spending so much time with me in da pantry. You should be helping Mrs. Wolfe fix da clothes."

A sour look flashed across David's face. "No," he said bitterly. "Sewing is women's work! People always pick on me when they know I can sew."

J-P was surprised by the angry response. "Do you know how many Jewish men work as tailors in this city? Or own shops in da clothing business? Probably half da people who run this orphanage have a relative working in the needle trade. For a kid who can sew like this, it'll be easy to find a job. So don't tell me sewing's women's work! I work in a kitchen and stock da pantry to make my living, but I don't mind. Everyone has to do something to earn money. If you're lucky, you can do something you're good at."

CHAPTER 14

It was just after David started school again in January that J-P thought of a way he might be able to help his young friend get to Seattle. But Mrs. Freedman hadn't heard anything yet from anyone she'd written to, and J-P couldn't think of anything David could actually do to find his uncle if he got there. So he didn't say anything for a while. But then, at the end of January, Mrs. Freedman finally got a letter from someone in Seattle. The man who had written her hadn't been able to locate anyone named Danny Embury, but the news wasn't entirely bad.

"Far from it," Mrs. Freedman said. "In fact, I'd say we've gotten some very promising clues."

"What kind of clues?" David asked.

"Well, it seems there are several families in Seattle your Uncle Danny could be related to. We've been spelling his name E-M-B-U-R-Y, but that isn't necessarily correct, is it?"

David realized that was true. He'd never actually seen the name written down. He'd only heard his mother say it.

"We haven't found a Danny Embury, but there are five families in Seattle named Embree and two named Embery. He could be part of one of those families. There's even someone named Irving Embury who might be a relative. The man who wrote back from *The Jewish Voice* — it's the Jewish newspaper there — will try to find their addresses and then he'll send them to me. Once we've got them, I can start writing letters to those people and we'll see if any of them can tell us something about your uncle."

When David told J-P the news, J-P realized there was now something David could actually do if he got to Seattle. He could find these people and talk to them himself. It was time to tell David what he'd been thinking.

The Stanley Cup final was going to be in the west this year, and if the Canadiens won the NHL title, they'd be the ones facing the championship team from the PCHA. There was no guarantee that team would be Seattle, but there were only three teams in that league, too, and Seattle was always a top contender. A job with a tailor or in a clothing store would probably make more sense for David in the long run, but there was plenty of time for that later. Right now a job mending uniforms for the Canadiens might help him find his uncle.

"Remember when I told you my bruder used to wrestle for Mr. Kennedy?" J-P asked David. "Well, he doesn't know me at all, but I'm sure as a favour to Jacques he'd meet with me."

"About what?"

"About you. Maybe if I talk to him and explain, he'd give you a job. Dere must be someone who has to sew up da holes players get in their uniforms."

"Do you really think he'll hire me?"

"I don't know. But I do know one thing. He'll probably see me because he liked my bruder, and he might even agree to meet with you, but dere's no way he'll give you a job just because of Jacques. Mr. Kennedy never does anything unless it makes sense ... Dollars and cents. So you'll have to show him you can do da job ... if dere's even a job to do."

J-P shook his head. "I wish I made you help Mrs. Wolfe after you fixed my coat. Then you could've been sewing all this time. But dere's nothing we can do about that. You'll just have to start now ... even if da other boys pick on you for it."

David and J-P spoke to Mrs. Freedman about their plan. They showed her how well he'd fixed J-P's coat, and she agreed that if David was going to quit school to start working in the fall, anyway, he might as well begin working now if J-P could get him this job. Privately, she never thought it would happen, but she also didn't see any harm in trying.

"You should keep going to school for now," she told David, "but if you think it'll help you to assist Mrs. Wolfe with the sewing, I'm sure she'd be glad to have you lend a hand."

So every day after school for the next few weeks, David helped Mrs. Wolfe whenever there was sewing to do. Some of the boys thought it was strange, but no one ever bothered to make any trouble. Boys and girls all had to do the dishes after dinner and take turns sweeping the floors in their dorms. No one really cared who did what as long as everything got taken care of.

With only three teams in the NHL, the regular season was just eighteen games long. It lasted only two months and was over by the middle of February. Two teams made the playoffs, and their series started one week later.

The Canadiens went on a hot streak in January, and they clinched a playoff spot before the end of the month. Although the Habs slumped subsequently, J-P paid Mr. Kennedy a visit after the team played its final game on February 15. Mr. Kennedy made no promises, but he agreed to meet with David at the Canadiens' practice on Friday before the playoffs started on Saturday, February 22.

The Canadiens always held their workouts at noon, so David had to skip school to attend the practice. He was going to drop out soon enough, anyway, so what did it matter?

J-P had to be at the Home to assist with lunch, so David had to go to the rink alone. He caught the streetcar at Saint Lawrence at ten o'clock to make extra sure he wouldn't be late. He arrived at Jubilee Rink shortly before eleven. The door was open, so he went inside.

There was no lobby inside the rink as there had been at Westmount Arena. Instead the doors opened right into the playing area. David stood just inside the door. He was pretty much in the exact same place where he and J-P had stood to watch the game. There were no players on the ice yet, but there were a couple of workmen. They were patching up a couple of ruts with a bucket of snow and a pail of water.

After a little while, David heard the door open behind him.

"Excusez-moi," a man said as he walked past David.

David looked over. He recognized the man right away. It was Georges Vézina!

During the next few minutes, the rest of the players arrived, too. All these men he'd read about in the newspapers and seen pictures of were walking right past him! They were close enough that he could say hello ... if he hadn't felt too nervous to do it! Most of them hurried by to get to the dressing room. Newsy Lalonde actually smiled at David as he walked by. He seemed much smaller in real life than David had expected. Joe Hall, too. They were both much smaller than Didier Pitre.

David was beginning to wonder if Mr. Kennedy was really going to be there when all of a sudden a pack of men entered the rink. David had seen pictures of Mr. Kennedy in the newspaper and picked him out immediately. As a former wrester himself, Mr. Kennedy was much larger than most of his hockey players. Of course, the expensive fur-and-leather winter coat he was wearing made his big body seem even bulkier than it was. He also had a wide moon face that seemed much rounder under the bowler hat he wore.

Mr. Kennedy spotted David as he came inside and realized who he must be. "Give me a minute, will ya, boys?" David heard him say to the reporters around him. "I gotta take care of something first. I'll meet you by the bench in a couple of minutes and we'll talk."

The men made their way around the rink, and Mr. Kennedy motioned for David to come over. "You're the kid Jean-Patrice talked to me about, right? Danny or David, or something?"

"David, sir. David Saifert."

"Have a seat, kid. Might as well get a good one. The team will be out on the ice pretty soon. You can watch them practise for a bit."

David Saifert followed Mr. Kennedy around the ice surface and sat behind the bench where he'd indicated.

"J-P tells me you're a whiz with a needle and thread," Mr. Kennedy said. "I'll bring you a sweater in a few minutes and we'll see what you can do. But first I have to speak to the gentlemen of the press." Mr. Kennedy looked over at the group of newspapermen waiting for him. Then he looked back at David and winked. "Gotta give 'em something to write about."

"What do you think, George?" David heard one of the newsmen ask Mr. Kennedy. "Ottawa's had your number lately. Can the Canadiens turn it around?"

"Can and will, boys," Mr. Kennedy said confidently. "We wrapped up a playoff spot early. There hasn't been anything for the team to play for lately. Now there is."

One of the reporters didn't seem convinced. "It can't be as simple as that, George. You've only had one win against Ottawa the last four times you've played them. The Senators whipped you 7–0 just last week. Now you've got to beat them four times in seven games. You really think the team can turn it around just like that?"

Mr. Kennedy smiled. "Can and will, boys. Ottawa's got a good team — don't get me wrong — but ours is better. We'll beat them, and I'll tell you what. We'll go out west and we'll beat whichever team we have to face there, too. We'll bring the Stanley Cup back to Montreal this year, boys. Just watch." He waved his arms toward the ice surface. As if on cue, Newsy Lalonde led his teammates out and began putting them through their paces.

David had never seen NHL players perform when the arena was empty. It was a lot different without the roar of the crowd. David could actually hear the sounds as their skate blades cut into the ice. *Crunch! Crunch! Crunch!* Tingles went up and down his spine. David was always amazed at how fast the players moved. The Canadiens weren't called "The Flying Frenchmen" for nothing, and few men in all of hockey were as speedy as Lalonde.

He watched Lalonde dash up the ice and close in on an unsuspecting player. When Lalonde was right behind the man, he lifted the player's stick and stole the puck. Then he shifted his weight so quickly that it looked as if he'd fall over. Instead, he spun gracefully and raced off in the opposite direction.

As David watched Newsy flip a soft shot at Georges Vézina — there was no point in wearing out the team's only goalie in practice! — Mr. Kennedy returned with the damaged sweater. "Joe Hall's," he said.

David's face went blank.

"Don't worry, kid. We've washed all the blood out." Mr. Kennedy chuckled as he tossed the sweater into David's lap.

Was he joking? David picked up the sweater and studied it. If there had been blood on the sweater, it wasn't there now.

"There's a tear in the left shoulder," Mr. Kennedy told him.

David spotted it. He could fix that easily.

"Follow me, kid. You can't sew properly sitting here in the stands. Your hands will freeze. There's a maintenance room around back with a stove to keep it warm."

David smiled when he saw it was the maintenance room he and J-P had climbed into that night. Even the stepladder was sitting in the same place against the wall. David hoped that was a sign his luck would be good again. Or was it an omen that he was going to be punished because he'd done something bad by sneaking in without paying?

He sat on the stool in front of the workbench and took out his sewing kit.

"There should be some of the proper red thread in the top drawer," Mr. Kennedy said.

David opened the drawer and pulled out a spool.

"Okay, kid, go to it. That's why you're here. I'll be back in a little while to see how you've done."

After Mr. Kennedy left him to do his work, David looked more carefully at the tear in Hall's sweater. It was really more of a hole than a tear. The simplest thing to do would be to stitch the hole closed, but that would make the fabric pucker a bit. It wouldn't be nice and smooth anymore. David knew it would be better to use a darning stitch. Darning was a process of weaving over a worn-out portion.

David pushed his needle into the sweater a little above the hole and began working down. He was careful to weave over and under the proper threads in the sweater. Then he pulled the thread in his needle across the space of the hole and back into the sweater again on the other side. He carried his weave a little beyond the other end of the hole, then turned and worked his way upward, careful to pass under the threads he'd worked over while coming down and over the threads he'd worked under!

He went back and forth across the hole in that up-and-down fashion until he'd covered the entire thing. But he wasn't done yet. Next he turned the sweater sideways and worked the same series of stitches back and forth across the patch he'd made until he did a complete weave over the hole. It took a lot longer to do it like that, but when he was finished the hole had been filled in perfectly.

Mr. Kennedy returned to the maintenance room just as David was wrapping up. Another man was with him.

"Well, let's see it," Mr. Kennedy said. David handed him the sweater, and the owner-manager inspected it carefully. He nodded. "Looks good. Real good. What do you think, Al?"

Mr. Kennedy passed the sweater over to the man who had come in with him. Al gave David a hard look, but when he checked the sweater he also nodded. "It is good. Better than I could do."

David smiled.

"But he's kinda scrawny," Al added.

Mr. Kennedy grinned. "What he means, kid, is that it's a lot of hard work if we hire you. There's no job just sewing. In fact, the players usually take care of any problems with their sweaters and socks themselves. Or their wives do, anyway."

David's face clouded.

"Then again, if we do go out west, we'll be on the road for almost a month and it would be nice to have someone who can keep the uniforms looking nice for the Stanley Cup playoff. But we still have to know you can do the whole job. So I'll tell you what. Why don't you come down here tomorrow before the game? Get here by five o'clock, and Al will put you to work. Then we'll know if you're any good."

"I'll do whatever you tell me. I can do the work. You'll see!" David was so excited he could hardly wait to tell J-P the news.

"But listen, kid, I know you heard me boasting to those reporters out there about how we'll beat Ottawa. Truth is, though, I'm worried. The Senators have been playing much better than us down the stretch, and they may well beat us. Your friend Jean-Patrice told me why you want to go to Seattle so badly, but we might not get the chance. We might not win. And even if we do — and even if you prove you can do the job — there's still no guarantee we'll take you with us. It'll mostly depend on the deals we can make with the railways and the hotels. We're not going to take any more people on this western trip than we can afford. You understand me?"

CHAPTER 15

David was determined to do whatever it took to show Al and Mr. Kennedy he could do the job. He left the Home at 3:30 on Saturday afternoon and arrived at the Jubilee at 4:20. Like the day before, he had to make the ride alone. J-P wouldn't be able to leave his job as the Shabbas Goy until after 6:15. The sun was setting much later now that it was the end of February. J-P was going to come down in time for the game and see if he could buy a ticket. With David in the rink it would probably be easy for him to put the ladder outside the window, but there was no way they were going to risk David's chance at the job like that. If J-P could get a ticket, he'd meet up with David after the game. If not, they'd meet back at his sister's. Once again David would have to spend the night there because there was no chance he'd be back at the Home by lights out.

He expected to walk into the Jubilee the way he'd done on Friday, but the rink was kept locked until seven o'clock on game days. There was a man at the door to let people in … but he didn't speak English!

David tried to explain. "*Mees-yure* Kennedy told me to be here."

"*Monsieur Kennedy n'est pas là,*" the man at the door said. "'Ee's not 'ere."

"No," David said. "He told *me* to be here."

The man shook his head.

"What about Al?" David asked. "Is Al here? *Un homme* named Al?"

"*Je ne parle pas anglais,*" the man said. "*Je ne comprends pas.*" And he closed the door.

David wasn't sure what to do next. Hopefully, Al would come searching for him at five o'clock. But what if he didn't? David could lose this job before he even had a chance to get it. Maybe he should go to J-P's sister and see if Maurice could come back with him and translate?

As David was thinking it over, a cab pulled up in front of the rink and another man got out. "Keep it running," he heard the man say. "I'll be back in a minute."

David had never heard the voice before — he would have expected it to sound more rumbling and mean — but he had no trouble recognizing the face. It was Joe Hall! The defenceman would be able to get David inside the rink, but he wasn't sure he could summon up the courage to speak to him. To his amazement Hall spotted him and said something first. "Are you the boy who fixed my sweater yesterday?"

David stared for a moment. "Yes, sir," he finally squeaked out.

Joe smiled. He knew that when most people met him the first time they expected him to be some kind of ogre. Off the ice, though, his personality was completely different. "You did a great job. Al mentioned you'd be helping tonight. Whatcha doing out here?"

"The man at the door wouldn't let me in. I guess he didn't understand what I was saying."

"Well, come in with me and I'll find Al for you."

Joe knocked at the door. The man opened it again and nodded at Joe. But then he glared at David.

"C'est bon," Joe said. "Il est avec moi."

The man shrugged and let them both in.

David followed Joe around the rink to the Canadiens' dressing room.

"Hey, Al!" Joe shouted as they got closer. "Al? Where are you?"

Al popped his head out from the dressing room door. "What are you doing here so early, Joe?"

"I'm gonna grab my skates and take 'em over to Art's shop to get sharpened. I gotta a taxi waiting for me out front ... Oh, and I brought someone for you."

Al saw David behind Joe. "You're early, too. Good. There's a lot to do. Follow me and we'll get started."

David followed Al into the dressing room. Considering how plain Jubilee Rink was, the Canadiens' dressing room was pretty nice. The man who had owned the Montreal Wanderers at the time had built the Jubilee back in 1909. He had intended for his team to play there — which it did for a while — so he had made sure the home dressing room was a good one. It had a wooden floor that wouldn't dull skate blades too much, and wooden stalls for the players around the wall.

In each of the stalls were pegs and a hanger. Beside each one was a skinny metal locker for clothes. There was a wooden chair in front of each one for the player to sit on. Above each stall was a slate board with a player's name and number written neatly in chalk. David looked around and spotted them all:

1. Vézina
2. Corbeau
3. Hall
4. Lalonde
5. Pitre
6. Cleghorn
7. Malone
8. Berlinquette
9. Couture
10. McDonald

It was hard to believe that within the next hour or so they would all be in there, talking and joking and getting ready for the game.

"First thing we gotta do," Al said, jerking his thumb at a door on the far wall, "is get all the gear out of the back." David followed him across the dressing room. "The smell can be a little hard to take at first," Al warned as he opened the door and led David through.

David winced as the tangy odour of stale sweat hit his nose hard enough to make his eyes water.

Al laughed. "Just breathe through your mouth a bit. You'll get used to it soon enough."

The smell came from the players' uniforms and equipment, which hung from cords strung like clotheslines.

"Everything's organized by the players' numbers. You gotta make sure you keep it all together or it's too hard to tell whose is whose. And believe me, the players will get angry if you mix it up. They all got their patterns and superstitions, and they get plenty cheesed off if you mess them up. So we always do everything the same way. The sweaters and socks get hung on the hanger inside the stalls. The underwear and other stuff go on hooks in the lockers. Pile the pads on the chairs and put the skates on the floor inside the stalls. Sticks get lined up on the wall by the door. And don't get any of them crossed! The guys think it's bad luck. Cleghorn goes crazy if he sees crossed sticks. Of course, it doesn't take much to make him go crazy. He's not as bad as his brother, though. Those Cleghorns both got a temper like Joe Hall at his worst."

Odie Cleghorn was new to the team this year, but he'd been a top player since 1910. For years he and his brother, Sprague, had starred together with the Montreal Wanderers. The war had kept Odie out of action during the first year of the NHL, and now that the Wanderers were gone, Odie was scoring goals for the Canadiens while Sprague was anchoring the defence in Ottawa. They'd be battling against each other in the playoffs. Sprague was the real wild one, but Odie could mix it up, too. Still, it was Joe Hall who had led the NHL in penalty minutes two years in a row.

As David carried the equipment into the dressing room, he realized he'd never given much thought to what the players wore for protection. It was amazing how little there was! Skinny leather pads lined with felt to cover their knees and shins. Pants made of canvas with wooden dowels sewn in to protect their thighs and butt. Nothing but extra layers of felt sewn into their undershirts to protect their shoulders and elbows. How did they hit each other so hard with equipment as flimsy as that? Only their leather gloves seemed sturdy enough to give decent protection. The sticks were solid and sturdy, too … yet they hit each other over the head with them and nobody wore a helmet!

When David was finished getting all the equipment, Al told him that if he got the job, one of his responsibilities would be to maintain the fire in the coal stove that kept the dressing room warm.

"It's only gotta be warm enough to take the chill off," Al said. "You make it too hot, and it's trouble. The last thing you want is for the guys to work up a sweat getting their gear on in the dressing room and then have their muscles freeze up when they go out into the cold. Guys can get hurt when that happens. Or catch pneumonia or something. You know how to work a coal-burning stove?"

David hesitated. Should he say that he did? But then he decided it would be worse to lie. He shook his head.

"There's nothing to it, really. You start it up with some paper and kindling, then throw a few logs in. Once they really get going, you just add the coal. When you do, you gotta make sure the draft's fully open. Afterward you can shut it down some. But you know what? I'll usually be the one to start it. You'll be the one who has to come in a few times during the game to throw a bit more coal on so it doesn't burn out. Then, when the game's nearly over, you can toss in a whole bunch and really heat it up in here. I'll do it with you tonight, so you know how much to use. But after the game's over — and after you've hung up all the equipment in the back room and the players have left — you'll be the one to shovel the ash out from the bottom. Coal makes ten times as much ash compared to wood."

By 6:30 the players had all begun to arrive. As at practice the day before, Georges Vézina was the first to show up. He nodded at Al as he entered the dressing room, then looked David up and down. It was hard to read anything in his expression. Vézina peered into his stall, and when he saw that everything seemed to be in order, he slowly undressed and put on his long underwear.

"Never known anyone as quiet as he is," Al whispered to David as the goalie did a few leisurely stretches. "I'm pretty sure he understands English, but I've never heard him speak it. As far as I know, he only speaks French. And it's got to be something pretty important before he'll even speak that!"

The dressing room got noisier once the other players showed up. They all seemed to like joking around.

"Big game tonight, Joe," Bert Corbeau said. "You ready, old man?"

At thirty-six Joe Hall was one of the oldest players in hockey. "Readier than you'll ever be," he said to

Corbeau, his twenty-four-year-old defence partner.

"Hey, Odie," Bert said, "give us some dirt on your brother. What can we say to get him really riled up?"

"You don't want to get him riled," Odie Cleghorn said. "He gets better when he gets angry."

"Unlike you. You just get stupider!"

Things got more serious as game time approached. Newsy Lalonde was the coach of the team as well as the captain, and he had a few words for his teammates before they faced the Senators.

"These guys beat us 7–0 last week, and they beat Toronto 9–3 a couple of days ago. They won seven of their last eight games, and we've only won three. They think they're better than we are, and if we let them beat us again tonight, it's going to be even tougher for us to stop them when we go to Ottawa for the next one. We gotta show them we mean business. We gotta beat 'em tonight, and beat 'em bad!"

CHAPTER 16

Newsy Lalonde had the skill to back up his words with actions. He scored three goals, and the Canadiens shook off their late-season slump by blasting the Senators 8–4. Odie Cleghorn scored three in the next game at Ottawa, and the Canadiens won 5–3. Back at the Jubilee for game three, Lalonde scored five times. The Canadiens won 6–3 and took a three-games-to-nothing lead. The series seemed to be in the bag now, but the Senators weren't going down without a fight. They staved off elimination with a 6–3 win of their own in game four, and the series went back to Montreal. At home for game five Lalonde set the tone with an early goal. The Canadiens went on to a 4–2 victory that wrapped up the series.

Although Al had told him he'd done good work, the Canadiens didn't take David with them for the games in Ottawa. They let him come back for the home games, however, and he was there when they wrapped up the series on a Thursday night. The newspapers on Friday morning all reported that the Canadiens would leave for the West Coast on Monday, which would be March 10.

They'd be on a train to Vancouver, but nobody knew for sure if that was where they'd wind up. Vancouver and Seattle were the teams that had made the PCHA playoffs, but their series wasn't over yet. It wouldn't end until a few days after the Canadiens left Montreal. So not only did David have to wait a bit longer to find out if Mr. Kennedy would let him go, there was still a chance that even if he did go, he wouldn't make it to Seattle.

As Mr. Kennedy had told him, taking David on the trip would cost the team more money. It wasn't really a matter of being able to afford it. It was more a problem that the extra expenses would have to come out of what the team earned on their trip. Gate receipts from the Stanley Cup games were supposed to cover all their expenses and also provide the players with some bonus money. Any extra expenses meant that each player would wind up getting a smaller bonus, and it wasn't as if any of them earned very much money to begin with. NHL salaries only ranged from about $500 to $1,500. Winning the Stanley Cup could mean an extra $300 or so to each player. Even the loser's share would be about $200.

Mr. Kennedy knew the bonus money meant a lot to the players, so he thought it was only fair they be the ones to decide if David could come or not. The team was going to meet at two o'clock on Saturday afternoon to discuss the trip. That was when they'd make up their minds.

Instead of getting together at the rink, the meeting was at the Athletic Club that Mr. Kennedy owned downtown. He had organized the Club Athlétique Canadien in 1908 before there even was a Montreal Canadiens hockey team. Although Mr. Kennedy was actually an Irish Canadian, his club was mostly for French Canadians.

George Kennedy had been one of Canada's best wrestlers in the early 1900s, but his family was never happy that he took up the sport. His real name was actually George Kendall, but he changed his surname to Kennedy because of his family's disapproval. In 1903 Mr. Kennedy gave up going into the ring and started training and promoting other wrestlers instead. Wrestling was the main interest when the Athletic Club started in 1908, but soon Mr. Kennedy got involved in other sports, too.

By 1910 the Club had constructed a four-storey building on Saint Catherine Street a few blocks east of Saint Lawrence. It had a fancy gymnasium with all sorts of exercise equipment and room to hold two thousand fans to watch boxing or wrestling matches. There was also a billiards parlour filled with pool tables, a bowling alley with automatic pin-setting machines, a handball court, showers, a sauna, and a massage room. There was even a reading room stocked with newspapers and sports magazines from all across Canada and the United States.

Mr. Kennedy told David to be at the club at three o'clock. The meeting would be just about over by then, and that was when the players would make their decision.

David took the Saint Lawrence streetcar to Saint Catherine Street, then walked for about ten minutes to the block past Saint Hubert Street where the club was located. *Rue San t-Hubear,* the French people said. This was the French part of downtown.

When he got there, David was sent upstairs to where Mr. Kennedy had his office. His secretary was there, and she told him to go in.

The door to the office was big and heavy, but almost silent on its hinges as David pushed it open. Mr. Kennedy was sitting behind a large desk that faced the door. A few of the players were seated in chairs in front of him. Most of them were standing.

Getting up from his seat when he saw David come in, Mr. Kennedy said, "Ah, good, you're here." He motioned for David to join him at the front of the room. "There's one more thing we need to discuss," he told the players. "And this kid is it. I'm sure you all recognize him. He's been helping out in the dressing room lately, and Al tells me he's been doing a find job. Kid's name is David Saifert. And here's the situation ..."

Mr. Kennedy sat on the edge of his desk before he continued. "Some of you guys will probably remember a fellow named Jacques Montagne who used to wrestle for me." There were a few nods and murmurs of agreement. "You probably heard that Jacques got killed fighting in Belgium. Well, David's a friend of Jacques's brother, and he's lost some people, too. His father got killed in the war, as well, and his mother and sister died from the flu. He's got no family left in Montreal."

The owner-manager explained about David's uncle and how David hoped to find him in Seattle if the team could take him out there with them. "Now this isn't charity we're talking about. The kid's going to work for it. But it's not just my money that's going to be affected. It's yours, too. So we're all going to vote on it."

Mr. Kennedy got up off his desk. He put a big arm around David's shoulders and gave him a slight shove toward the door. "And you're going to wait downstairs until we're done. So go grab a newspaper or something in the reading room. I'll be down to let you know when the boys have decided."

———————

As the captain, Newsy Lalonde spoke first. "The kid works hard as far as I can tell. It's fine by me if we bring him along."

"That's easy for you to say," Billy Couture grumbled. "You make more money than any two of us put together!"

"Yeah, but what's it gonna cost to bring him?" Odie Cleghorn asked. "Another hundred bucks maybe? Even if it's $200, that's still only $20 off each of our bonuses."

"Says the guy whose father works in the oil business," Couture countered. "Twenty bucks is a lot of money to some of us! Jobs in the summer will be harder to find now that the soldiers are back. And what if Vancouver beats them and we don't even go to Seattle? Then it's $20 off our bonuses for nothing! Al was handling our equipment fine all season without him."

"Billy's right," Louis Berlinquette said. "And my wife's expecting a baby in the spring. We sure could use that bonus money."

Joe Hall shook his head with disgust. "I've got three kids of my own at home. My wife and I are both from big families, but if we weren't, I'd sure like to think there'd be someone who'd look out for them if something happened to us. This kid needs our help, and I think we should give it to him."

The room fell silent for a moment.

Then another player spoke. It was Georges Vézina. "I sayz we bring da boy," he told his teammates. "And dat we all help to pay. Even if we don't get to Seattle, it's da right t'ing to do."

Everyone stared at the goalie for a moment. Then

there were nods of agreement from around the room. Even Couture and Berlinquette weren't going to argue when the Silent Habitant spoke out in English.

"Okay then," Newsy announced. "It's decided. The kid can come."

CHAPTER 17

David was so excited after Mr. Kennedy gave him the news that he couldn't see himself sitting on a streetcar. So he part ran, part walked the two miles or so from the Athletic Club back to the Home. It was a little after four o'clock when he got there. At that time of day J-P was in the kitchen helping to get things ready for dinner. It was so obvious from the expression on David's face that the boy didn't have to tell him anything.

"Dey're going to take you!" J-P said.

David nodded excitedly.

"That's great!"

David couldn't remember if he'd ever hugged his father. Probably, when he was really little. But even when his father had left for the army, all they'd done was shake hands. Now David threw his arms around his friend.

"Thanks, J-P. Thank you so much. For everything."

"Ahh," J-P said, mussing up David's hair the way hockey players did when someone scored a goal, "I didn't do so much. You did it yourself. Now get outta here so I can get my work done!"

The next day was Sunday. Sundays were always rest-less days around the Home. Most of the kids were usually there, but a lot of the staff wasn't. Sundays were J-P's only day off, and since David had never become close to any of the other boys, he didn't want to just hang around. So he went outside and started walking. He didn't really know the best way to go, but he knew once he got to Saint Jo-seph Boulevard that if he kept walking he'd eventually hit Papineau Avenue. After that it would be like his old walk through the neighbourhood coming home from school.

David passed the blacksmith shop and the fire station and all the stores where his mother used to shop. After about an hour of walking, he finally reached Chabot. He stopped in front of the family's old building and glanced up at the flat on the third floor. David couldn't see anyone there, but he spotted other people's things on the landing. Still, standing there on the street, it was hard to believe that if he climbed those winding stairs his mother wouldn't be there waiting for him. But, of course, she wouldn't be. And yet he had gone there to talk to her.

"I'm going to Seattle," he said quietly. "I'm going to find Uncle Danny."

———————————

On Monday morning David told Mrs. Freedman the news. She made quick arrangements for the people who donated clothes to the Home to provide him with a new pair of pants, a few new shirts, and a suitcase. Mrs. Wolfe altered a man's suit jacket to fit him so that he'd have something nice to wear, as well.

Mrs. Freedman stayed late at the Home that night, and when it was time for David to go to the station, she took him there in a taxi. Then she handed him an envelope with a sheet of paper inside that had all the addresses from Seattle typed on it.

"Good luck," she said, and gave him a kiss on the cheek and a hug.

There was a tear in David's eye when he said, "Thank you."

Windsor Station looked like a castle on the southeast corner of Dominion Square in downtown Montreal. BETTER THAN ANYTHING EVER BUILT, a sign had said when the Canadian Pacific Railway station first opened back in 1889. Since then it had been made even bigger and better. Its main office tower now soared fifteen storeys above the street.

The Canadiens left Windsor Station for Vancouver on Train No. 1 of the Canadian Pacific's Transcontinental Line at 10:15 on Monday night, March 10, 1919. David hadn't had much time to get ready. Then again, there wasn't too much he needed to do.

A big crowd was at the station to cheer the Canadiens as they left to go after the Stanley Cup. Including David, there were twelve people travelling west with the team. Mr. Kennedy was going, of course, and Al was, too, but only nine of the team's ten players were making the trip. Joe Malone had decided not to go. With hockey salaries so low, Malone had decided to put the new job he had in his hometown of Quebec City ahead of the game. Except for the playoff trips to Ottawa, Malone had already skipped most of the Canadiens' road trips during the season, and he wasn't about to take a whole month off for this western trip ... even to play for the Stanley Cup.

Mr. Kennedy had arranged with the railway for the Canadiens to travel west in their own private sleeping car. It was first-class all the way and very snazzy! The twelve sets of double-sided bench seats were upholstered much more comfortably than in the regular sleeping cars. During the day, a table could be placed between the seats, and at night they pulled out into large beds with thick curtains for privacy. Above these lower berths were the upper berths. By day the upper berths were tucked closed and out of the way with metal bottoms so shiny they reflected the light coming through the windows as if they were mirrors. At night they folded down into smaller "top bunks" with a ladder for climbing up.

Veteran players always got the lower berths when

teams travelled by train. Younger players slept up top. David got an upper berth near the back. That was the space closest to the washrooms, which was convenient in some ways, but also meant that people were always passing by when they had to go.

Since the train left Windsor Station at 10:15 at night, the private car was already set up for sleeping when the Canadiens got onboard. Most of the players dropped off their bags and headed for the parlour car where they could sit up and talk or play cards until later in the night. But David climbed up into his berth, got into his pajamas, and tried to sleep. It was hard to get comfortable at first, because the train made so many stops and starts along the way, but when the locomotive finally opened up for a long run after midnight, the gentle rocking helped put David to sleep.

A little after seven o'clock in the morning two porters came through the car and quietly announced it was time to get up. There was a parade of people back and forth to the washrooms for the next little while as the players cleaned up and shaved, then went back to their berths to get dressed. David waited until everyone else was done before he got cleaned up. Then he dressed and made his way to the dining car to get some breakfast. It was pretty crowded when David got there, but he heard someone calling him.

"Over here. I saved you a seat."

It was Joe Hall. The defenceman nodded at one of the porters, who went to get David some breakfast. "Sit down," Joe said, patting the seat beside him. "I ordered you some bacon and eggs. Hope you don't mind. My oldest boy — Joe Junior — is about your age and that's what he likes in the morning."

David loved bacon, and he hadn't had any for a long time. There was only kosher food at the Home. "Thanks," he mumbled as the porter brought him his plate of food.

Except for J-P, David had never been very good around new people, and he just couldn't get used to the idea of being so close to Bad Joe Hall — even if the man really didn't seem very bad at all. So while David was glad to have the tasty breakfast, he mostly just stared out the window as he ate. It was fascinating to watch the scenery flying by.

"Ever been on a train before?" Joe asked.

David shook his head. "Been on the streetcar a lot, but this is better!"

Joe smiled as David turned to gaze out the window again. "Do you know where we are?" David asked after a while.

Joe looked out the window, too. He'd been back and forth on the train between Brandon and Quebec so many times over the years that he knew the route well.

"Can't say I really pay that much attention anymore, but it looks like we're still running alongside the Ottawa River, which means we haven't reached Mattawa yet." He checked his wristwatch. It was a little after 8:30. "We'll get there about nine o'clock and hit North Bay an hour later. They'll hook us up to a new locomotive there."

The big train engines had to be switched every 150 miles or so during the 2,886-mile trip from Montreal to Vancouver. Different locomotives were assigned to various sections along the route. The sturdiest ones were needed to pull the trains over the mountains. Railway workers also had to load on new coal and fresh water at many of the stops along the way to feed the fires that created the steam that powered the engines.

"You know," Joe said to David after the boy finished eating his breakfast. "I lost my father when I was only eight years old. Of course, I still had my mother, but she had seven of us to look after. She turned our place into a rooming house so she could work and still take care of us. Even so, I had to quit school when I was your age. Got a job in a cigar factory. I still work for them when the season's over, but not in the factory anymore. When I started getting famous as a hockey player, they figured I'd be more valuable as a salesman. Pay's pretty good, but it keeps me on the road an awful lot. Between that and hockey, I'm hardly ever at home with my wife and kids."

This was a private side of Joe Hall few people knew about. David wondered if Joe's frustration at the long times he had to spend away from his family was part of the reason his anger boiled over so often when he was on the ice. It was hard to believe a guy who could be so mean could be so nice.

———————

It was going to take the Canadiens six and a half days to get to Vancouver from Montreal. Even for David, every day on the train quickly became pretty much the same. People had to find something to do to occupy their time. All of the players had their routines.

David wasn't surprised to see Georges Vézina enjoying most of his time alone. In fact, he spent a lot of his days on the train sleeping. The goalie had brought some French magazines with him, but he only read them for a few minutes a few times each day.

"He worries about the strain on his eyes," Joe explained. "You can't stop the puck if you can't see it!"

As a forward, Jack McDonald had no such worries. Jack had been a big goal scorer in his early days, but now he was a trusted substitute coming off the bench when someone needed a rest. He had brought a couple of books with him and occupied most of his time with reading. Some of the players teased him about that. Most of them passed the time playing cards.

Billy Couture and Louis Berlinquette were substitutes, too. They stuck together and loved to play gin. Didier Pitre and Newsy Lalonde were the team's star players and had been on the club the longest, going all the way back to when the NHA was organized in 1909. They played poker with Al and Mr. Kennedy. Just small stakes, though. Their boss was a lot richer than they were.

Bert Corbeau also liked to play cards, but he was something of a loner. He figured the best way to be alone in a crowded railway car was to play solitaire. Odie Cleghorn, on the other hand, was the restless type. He liked to keep moving around the car in an effort to stay busy. Cleghorn would tease McDonald about his book reading and was always trying to get Couture and Berlinquette arguing about something. He kept tabs on the other card players, too.

"You can move that row under the red ten onto the black jack," he said, sliding into the seat next to Corbeau. "Oh, look at that!" he said excitedly as the removal of the ten turned up a red queen. "Now you can shift the whole thing back over onto the queen and then move up that black king you've got. Then you slide the pile over there."

Corbeau slammed down the cards in his hand. "I know how to play the game," he growled. "They call it solitaire for a reason, you know."

"Sorry, Bert," Cleghorn said. He got up to go, but his mischievous grin made it clear he wasn't sorry at all.

One of the ways everyone, except Georges Vézina, liked to pass the time was by reading the newspaper. The porters always brought several copies of the local papers onboard when they hit some of the bigger cities.

"Hey, George!" Newsy called out to Mr. Kennedy from behind a copy of the Winnipeg newspaper they'd picked up in a small town across the border in Manitoba. "Maybe the next time we make this trip you can rent us a couple of airplanes."

"What are you talking about, Lalonde?"

"Says here they're gonna fly those planes clear across the ocean pretty soon. Says Billy Bishop might make the first flight. If they can fly a plane across the ocean, it's gotta be easier to fly one across the country."

"You'll never get me up in one of those rickety crates," Mr. Kennedy said. "If the man upstairs wanted us to fly, he'd have given us wings."

The others laughed.

Sports was the usual topic of conversation when the players were reading stories out of their newspapers. Spring training was about to get started, and there was lots of news about baseball.

"Looks like Babe Ruth's gonna be a holdout," Newsy said.

"How much does he want?" Joe asked.

"A three-year deal for thirty thousand bucks. But he'll agree to take fifteen thousand for one year."

"Whew! That's a lotta dough! What do the Boston Red Sox say?"

Newsy squinted at the paper. "Owner's offering him eighty-five hundred for one year."

"Boy, imagine turning down that kind of money!"

"Story says he doesn't even want to pitch anymore. Just play the outfield."

Joe whistled. "But the guy's a twenty-game winner."

"I know, but he hit eleven home runs last year playing part-time in the outfield. Tied him for the American League lead."

"That's like Georges leading the league in scoring! Still, is he worth ten thousand bucks a year?"

"Says he'll quit baseball and take up boxing if he doesn't get it."

Joe grinned. "Big money in that."

"If you don't mind getting beat up for a living."

"Oh, like we don't get beat up?"

"But imagine if a guy as big as Babe Ruth was hitting you …"

"Knock you right out of the park!"

"He'd have to catch me first."

"Hah!"

CHAPTER 18

Joe Hall and David spent a lot of time together on the train. Most of the other players didn't pay much attention to him, but Joe seemed to like having him around. David figured it was probably because he missed his own kids.

Joe told David that most of the Canadiens were hoping to play Vancouver in the Stanley Cup series. "It's got nothing to do with you," he said. However, like their concerns about David, it did have to do with money.

"It's because the rink in Vancouver is so much bigger," Joe explained. "It's got nearly eleven thousand seats. Seattle's barely holds four thousand. That means the bonuses will be bigger if we play Vancouver because the money all comes from ticket sales."

In fact, the players' money only came from the ticket sales for the first three games. The Stanley Cup series was a best-of-five series, but officials from the two leagues didn't want the players dogging it. Paying them for only the first three games meant no one would try to lose on purpose so the series would go the limit and they'd make more money.

"But it doesn't really matter who any of us *wants* to play, does it?" Joe said. "Whatever happens is going to happen no matter what anyone wants. When the PCHA playoff wraps up on Friday, then we'll know."

The game on Friday started at 8:15 in Vancouver. It ended a little after ten o'clock. The Canadiens were on the train in Calgary, which meant it was shortly after eleven when word of the game reached them. A telegram was waiting for Mr. Kennedy at the station. A porter brought it to him in the car, and all the players gathered around as he took it. David had already climbed into his berth, but he certainly wasn't sleeping.

"It's Seattle, boys," Mr. Kennedy told them. "They won it 7–5."

David could hear some of the players groan at the news, but in his berth he fell asleep with a smile on his face.

"So you're going to Seattle," Joe said at breakfast the next morning. "You must be excited."

David *was* excited, but he knew better then to look too pleased with the other players around. He nodded and smiled shyly.

Joe hadn't asked David much about his uncle before.

He didn't want to get him talking about it in case he wasn't going to get the chance to go to Seattle. Now that he was, Joe was curious. "So what do you know about this uncle of yours?"

"Not too much," David admitted. "My mother used to tell me stories about him, but she hadn't seen him since he was younger than I am now. I'll show you ..." David had the picture of his Uncle Danny with his sewing kit in his suitcase, and he went back to get it.

Like everyone who saw it, Joe was amazed by the resemblance. "He looks just like you!"

"I know."

"So what happened to him? How come you don't know how to find him?"

David explained how his mother and her brother had both been sent to Canada and how a new family had adopted him but not her. "When they were all living in Montreal, my mother got to see him a lot. She said his new family was always nice to her, but they didn't want to adopt a teenage girl. Even after they moved all the way to Vancouver, my mother and my uncle still wrote to each other. But then Mr. Embury — Danny's father — got sick and he had to go to a special hospital in Seattle. My mother said that Danny and his mother moved there to be close to him, but then he died. She said after that the letters stopped coming."

David also told Joe about Mrs. Freedman and the letters she'd written and the addresses she'd been sent and how maybe Embury was really Embery or Embree. "There's only eight addresses altogether. I'm going try to find those people and talk to them. Maybe one of them will know where my uncle is."

But David had never told anyone the whole story before now. All that J-P and Mrs. Freedman had known was that David had an uncle named Danny Embury and that he lived in Seattle. When Joe heard the whole story, he realized that if Danny's mother had gotten remarried after her husband died, then she wouldn't be Mrs. Embury anymore. Danny's family name might have changed, too. While there was still a chance that one of those families might know something, Joe was worried that David might have come all this way and wouldn't really be looking for the right person.

CHAPTER 19

As the train rumbled through the Rocky Mountains on Saturday afternoon, another telegram arrived for Mr. Kennedy during the long stopover to change locomotives at the station in Golden, British Columbia. This telegram confirmed when the games were going to be played in Seattle. After he talked about it with the players, Mr. Kennedy sat with David. "We're going to get into Vancouver tomorrow morning," he told him.

"When will we get to Seattle?" David asked.

"Well, we're going to rest up in Vancouver for a bit. Then on Monday, after supper, we'll board the overnight steamship. When we wake up on Tuesday, we'll be in Seattle."

David smiled, though his head shook in disbelief.

"Here's the schedule," Mr. Kennedy said, handing the telegram to David.

SERIES STARTS 19TH (WED).
OTHER GAMES AS FOLLOWS:
GM 2 SAT 22

3 MON 24
4 WED 26
5 SAT 29

"As you can see, if the series goes the limit, we'll play five games in eleven nights."

The nineteenth to the twenty-ninth only looked like ten days, but David counted on his fingers while Mr. Kennedy was talking. It really was eleven days.

"If it wraps up early, we'll play some exhibitions game in Vancouver and Victoria to make a few extra bucks. So you might have as little as a week in Seattle, and certainly no more than two."

David could see that once again what was best for him wasn't what was best for the players. They stood to make more money from the trip if they won the Cup quickly. David wanted as much time in Seattle as he could get.

"I know you've got things you want to do there," Mr. Kennedy said, "but I told the boys you'd be working to earn your keep. So when we need you, you're going to work. It'll be busy the first couple of days, but after that Al will handle the practices himself and you can do what you've got to do. But on game days I'll expect you to be around. Understand?"

David nodded. "Yes, sir."

———————

It was still winter when the team left Montreal. A couple of feet of snow had been on the ground, and though the weather was warming up the temperature hadn't been above freezing for months. Along most of the route west winter was apparent, but when the team arrived on the coast it was definitely spring.

"It's hardly ever cold out here," Joe told David when the team got off the boat in Seattle on Tuesday morning. "Something about the way the mountains trap the warm air coming off the Pacific Ocean. Of course, it also makes it rain a lot, too."

As if on cue, it began to drizzle.

Everyone put down their things in order to turn up the collars on their overcoats. Everyone except David. His load was too awkward to lower. Each player carried a suitcase, and a canvas duffle bag stuffed with hockey gear. Mr. Kennedy didn't have any equipment, but he'd brought two suitcases. Al was lugging his own suitcase plus David's. David was carting the players' hockey sticks bundled up in his two outstretched arms. They'd been tied together with ropes at either end, which made it a lot easier. That was good because he was having trouble keeping his mind on what he was carrying.

David kept looking all around. If his uncle was in Seattle somewhere, there was a chance that any man he passed could be him.

Well, not any man.

David knew that his uncle was about five years younger than his mother. That meant he'd be about thirty years old now. With dark brown hair and light blue eyes. Like his. Would he really be able to pick him out if he saw him?

"Hey! Watch where you're going, kid!"

It was Billy Couture. David had nearly run into him when the players stopped in front of a taxi stand.

"Lay off him, Bill," Joe said calmly. "He's just excited we're here."

"Doesn't mean he shouldn't watch where he's going."

Mr. Kennedy had arranged for three big cars to meet the team. They pulled up before any more harsh words were exchanged and everyone piled in.

The team was staying at the Georgian Hotel, which was at 1420 Fourth Street in the heart of Seattle's business district. It was only a short ride to there from the waterfront, but it was long enough for David to see that Seattle was a much newer city than Montreal.

Seattle had been founded in the 1850s. With the many forests that surrounded the area, the city became an important lumber town and grew quickly. Even a terrible fire that destroyed the downtown in 1889 couldn't slow Seattle's growth. In fact, the downtown was rebuilt with structures of brick and stone to replace the burned-out wooden buildings.

More and more money poured into Seattle after gold was discovered in the Klondike during the summer of 1896. There was no gold in Seattle, but by 1897 it had become the main transport centre and supply depot for the fortune-seekers who sailed north to Alaska and the Yukon. Shipbuilding soon replaced lumber as the city's biggest industry, and Seattle kept growing into the 1900s. Shipbuilding had been more important than ever during the war, so Seattle had continued to prosper.

David knew none of the history of the city, but he could certainly see its effects. Unlike the narrow streets of Montreal, the roads in Seattle were wide and smooth. The downtown buildings were tall and impressive. The Smith Tower near the harbour stood an incredible forty-two storeys high! Except for some of the mighty skyscrapers of New York City, the Smith Tower was the tallest building in the world.

No other building in Seattle could approach the Smith Tower for height, but there were many others that were equally impressive in different ways. The Cobb Building was down the block from the Canadiens' hotel. It was only eleven storeys high, but its beautiful red brick with white plaster embellishing the top and bottom floors made it a marvel just the same. Across the street were three other fancy structures known collectively as the White-Henry-Stuart Building. Together they filled an entire city block. David had to crane his neck to stare up at them through the window of the taxi as they drove by.

But for all of Seattle's man-made beauty nothing matched its natural surroundings. The waters of Puget Sound were on one side of the city and Lake Washington was on the other. To the south there was Mount Rainier. Although it rained a lot in Seattle, the view of this snowcapped ancient volcano rising above the city on a clear day was spectacular. People in Montreal called Mount Royal a mountain, but it wasn't even eight hundred feet high. It was really a big hill. Mount Rainier was more than fourteen thousand feet high!

Like so many other buildings in the city, Seattle Arena was something special, too. It was probably the nicest rink in all of North America. From the outside it looked nothing like a warehouse or a factory as so many other arenas did. The bricks were pale yellow and the roof copper green. There were large arch-shaped windows all around the arena, and the ones above the entrance were outlined in white.

Inside, the rink was even nicer. There were only seats around three sides of Seattle Arena, but they weren't made of wood as in most other rinks. They were padded the way they were in a theatre. And it was warm inside, too. Because of the mild weather on the West Coast, Seattle Arena needed artificial ice. Refrigerated pipes running beneath the floor kept the ice hard, not freezing temperatures. That meant coal didn't have to be fed into a stove in the dressing room, either. If it ever did get too cold inside, the rink had electric heat to warm things up.

Located on Fifth Avenue between Seneca Street and University, Seattle Arena was two blocks from the Georgian Hotel. The Canadiens had a practice at noon, so Al took David over to the rink with him early to set up. It didn't take long to unload the equipment from the duffle bags and hang it up in the lockers, but it took more time to get everyone's skates sharpened. David couldn't help with that, so while Al handled the skates, he inspected the uniforms. With so much time to kill on their travels, David had made any necessary repairs to the players' uniforms on the train. Still, he checked them again. Everything looked good.

Twelve days had passed since the Canadiens had wrapped up their playoff series with Ottawa, so Newsy Lalonde put the team through a hard workout when they hit the ice. Once word got around that the Canadiens were inside, the rink began to fill up with fans. After a while, there was a pretty good crowd.

This wasn't the first time the Canadiens had visited Seattle. The Montreal team had faced the Mets —

Seattle's team name, short for Metropolitans — two years earlier. The 1917 series had been a disaster for the Canadiens. They won the first game 8–4 but then lost the next three in a row. The Mets beat them 6–1 and 4–1 before wrapping up the series with a crushing 9–1 victory. Seattle fans wanted to get a look at this year's Canadiens to see what their favourites would be up against this time.

David also sat in the stands, watching the practice with Al and Mr. Kennedy. As the workout wound down, David noticed a man approaching them. He was well dressed in a jacket and tie with an elegant overcoat and matching cap. As he got closer, David saw that he was quite short but had big jug ears.

Mr. Kennedy smiled as the man reached them, then stood to shake his hand. "Royal Brougham of the *Seattle Post-Intelligencer*."

"At your service," the reporter said with a little bow. "Mind if I ask you a few questions, George?"

"I'd be disappointed if you didn't!"

Brougham pulled out a notebook and pencil from a pocket in his coat and took a seat in the stands beside Mr. Kennedy. He got straight to business. "I imagine you're expecting to make a better showing this time around."

"Indeed. We're anxious to avenge our defeat. The team's a lot better than it was two years ago."

"Pete Muldoon's making no secret of his plans for the series. He says he'll send out his boys to skate your guys off their feet."

Mr. Kennedy chuckled. "We're pretty fast, too."

"Not fast enough last time."

"Look, we know Seattle has one of the fastest teams in the history of hockey and we know they'll give us a battle, but I think we'll turn the tables on them this time. My boys have never played as well as they're doing now."

"So you think you can outskate 'em?"

Mr. Kennedy flashed a sly smile. "I'd say we can match your speed better than you can match our muscle. Joe Hall might be one of the oldest players in the game, but he's still the best defenceman in hockey and wields a pretty mean stick, too! And Corbeau, his partner, tips the scales at nearly two hundred pounds. We'll see how fast Frank Foyston and Jack Walker are moving once Bert starts throwing his weight around."

"So what's your prediction for the series?"

"Well, let's just say I'm expecting to win tomorrow night."

But Mr. Kennedy was wrong. Not only did the Canadiens lose, they weren't even close. Seattle won the first game 7–0.

CHAPTER 20

Although the newspapers said the game was closer than the score made it seem — Vézina had a terrible night, while Seattle goalie Hap Holmes stopped at least six sure goals — David was glad to get out of everyone's way on Thursday morning. The players had been pretty angry on Wednesday night and cleared out of the dressing room as quickly as they could. David stayed late to help clean up, but as Mr. Kennedy had promised, Al would now take care of things by himself when the club held practices.

With game two not scheduled until 8:30 on Saturday night, David had the next two and a half days to search for his uncle. Even the weather seemed to co-operate. After two days of rain, the sun was shining on Thursday morning and the temperature was the warmest yet.

David had gotten a copy of the *Seattle Street and Car Line Guide* at the hotel. Using that, he'd been able to figure out where most of the addresses on his list were located and how to get to them. Only one address had him confused. Benton Embree, a lawyer, had his home address listed as Pontiac Lake. His work address said 417 New York Block. David asked the man at the front desk of the hotel about those.

"Pontiac Lake?" the clerk said. "I don't know Pontiac Lake. You must mean Pontiac Bay near the top of Lake Washington. There are some pretty fancy homes on Sand Point up there. That would make sense if this man's a lawyer."

David flipped through his guidebook. "I don't see it. Do you know how to get there from here?"

"The streetcar lines don't run that far. There's a train that runs out past there a couple of times a day, though. The King Street Station's not too far from here. You can probably walk it in twenty minutes or so."

"What about the New York Block? What's that?"

The clerk smiled. "It's an office building, and it's only about ten minutes from here."

The clerk gave David directions, which were simple. He only had to walk west to Second Avenue and then go south a few blocks to Cherry Street. "It's not too far from the Smith Tower," the man explained. "As long as that's still in front of you, you haven't gone too far."

Dressed in his new pair of pants, his best shirt, and the suit jacket Mrs. Wolfe had tailored for him, David headed into the sunshine. Staring up at the buildings he saw and into the faces of the men he passed, it took him more time than the clerk had told him, but it still didn't take long to reach his destination.

The New York Block was a seven-storey office building as wide as it was tall. It had been one of the first brick-and-stone buildings built after the horrible downtown fire of 1889. Many prettier buildings had gone up in the thirty years since then, but the New York Block still looked sturdy and important.

David climbed the stairs to the sixth floor. His heart was pounding when he got to the top. It was more from excitement than from exercise. What if Benton Embree was his Uncle Danny? David knew that wasn't likely, but maybe the man would at least be able to tell him something.

He found the door to number 417 and went inside. A woman was working at a typewriter in the small front room. There was a door to a larger office behind her desk.

"Can I help you?" she asked.

David's throat was suddenly dry. He didn't want to sound like a shy little boy when he spoke, so he swallowed hard first. "I'd like to speak to Mr. Embree."

"Do you have an appointment?"

"Uh, no."

"I'm Mr. Embree's secretary, and I'm afraid he's very busy right now. But perhaps he'll have some time to see you this afternoon ... if you'll tell me what this is regarding."

David had had a lot of time on the train to think about what he was going to say if he got to Seattle. He swallowed hard again and then started to explain. "My name's David Saifert, and I'm trying to find someone here in Seattle. A man named Embury ... or maybe Embree. I don't really know, but he's my uncle and I need to find him. I've come all the way from Montreal ..."

He told her about the war and the Spanish Flu and how they had made him an orphan. He explained about his mother and her brother and showed the woman the photograph.

When he was done, the woman got up and opened the door to the larger office. As she went in, David heard her say, "Mr. Embree, there's a boy out here I think you should see," before she closed the door behind her. A few minutes later she came out again and told David he could go in.

Benton Embree was a pleasant-looking man. To David he seemed old. He was probably in his mid-fifties, but his balding head made him look even older. Like so many wealthy men, he was a little chunky but not really fat.

"Hello, David," Mr. Embree said, holding out his hand for David to shake. He then motioned toward the chair in front of his desk and David sat down. Mr. Embree took his seat behind the desk. "Miss Carter, my secretary, told me your story. It's quite remarkable that you've managed to get yourself all the way out here. Do you wish to hire me to help find your uncle? That's not really what I do."

"No, sir. I only thought that maybe you'd know something about him or his family. That maybe you're related to them."

"Tell me again why you think he's in Seattle?"

David explained about Danny's family moving west and then coming to Seattle when his father got sick.

Mr. Embree shook his head. "My wife and I moved to Seattle in 1898. Our son, Harold, was born the next year. We don't have any other family here, and I've never known anyone named Daniel Embree. I'm sorry."

David nodded slowly.

"Is there anything else I can do for you?"

"I don't think so."

"What will you do now?"

"Well, sir, I have a list of eight families. I'm going to try to talk to them all. Maybe someone will know something."

Mr. Embree stood. "May I see your list?"

David handed it to him.

"Some of these are a long way from here. How are you planning to get to them all?"

"On the streetcar."

Mr. Embree sat down again and thought for a moment. "Hmm." Then he smiled. "If you can be back here tomorrow morning at nine o'clock, I'll arrange for a driver to take you around to the rest of the addresses on your list. I'll also have Miss Carter type up a letter for each one of these families. If no one's at home, you can leave a letter for them. It will instruct them to contact this office if they have any information about your uncle."

CHAPTER 21

"Howdy, stranger," Joe said to David when he saw him at the hotel on Saturday. "How's it been going the past couple of days?"

David told Joe about Mr. Embree. Of course, he'd been able to go back to the man's office on Friday morning, and with the car he was able to visit all seven addresses in just a few hours. There was no one home at three of his stops, so he left them the letters that Miss Carter had typed. He spoke to someone at each of the other four houses, but no one knew anything about his uncle.

"Mr. Embree said he'll telephone the hotel if anyone has any information. If something happens after we've left, he'll send a telegram to Mrs. Freedman at the Home."

"Sounds like a nice man," Joe said.

"Yeah."

"So what are you going to do now?"

David shrugged. "Nothing, I guess. Just wait and see ... and help out more with the team."

He had never really had a plan beyond talking to the families on the list. David had always figured one of them would know something about his Uncle Danny. Maybe one of them would somehow be him, only with a different first name for some reason. But Joe still felt it was much more likely that if David's uncle had a different name it would be a different last name.

"Go get that picture of your uncle and come with me," Joe said. "I've got an idea."

"What kind of idea?"

"You'll see."

"Where are we going?"

"To talk with Royal Brougham."

The office of the *Seattle Post-Intelligencer* newspaper was across the street from the Georgian Hotel. Royal Brougham was at his desk on the third floor, typing up his preview story about game two.

"Hey, Joe, how are ya? I was just over at the hotel talking to Kennedy. He's counting on you guys to bounce back strong tonight. Can you do it?"

"Well, we're sure gonna try."

"Come on," the reporter teased. "Give me something more colourful than that! How are you boys really feeling? The Mets put quite a beating on you. What's the inside scoop?"

"Actually, I was hoping you might be able to do

something for me."

"Whatcha got in mind?"

"This boy," Joe said, tilting his head in David's direction, "has a story you might be interested in." He gave Royal a quick rundown of David's story.

"That's quite a tale," the reporter said, "but I'm not really the one to tell it. You're in luck, though. We got a girl downstairs name of Madge Bailey. She's in on Saturdays to write the fine arts column for the Sunday edition. You know, what shows are opening at the galleries and what the local artists are up to. That kind of stuff. She's always looking for something a little meatier to write about. Bet she'd love to get her teeth into this."

"Thanks, Royal. I owe you one."

"And don't think I won't be coming to collect it!"

David followed Joe down to the second floor to look for Madge Bailey. There weren't very many women in the newsroom, so it wasn't hard to find her. As Royal had suspected, she was very interested in David's story.

"The flu epidemic was awful here, too," Mrs. Bailey told them. "Just awful! It hit us much later than it did in the east, so we thought we knew what to do. Schools, churches, theatres ... they were all shut down. Everyone had to wear masks. But then the war ended and the flu seemed to stop back east. Not here, though. It just got worse and worse. November and December were the most terrible months of all. Schools didn't reopen until January, but things didn't really get back to normal until February. By then more than a thousand people had died, but finally now in March, thank goodness, there hasn't been a single death reported from influenza."

Like everywhere else, people in Seattle didn't want to hear about the Spanish Flu now that it seemed to be gone for good, but Mrs. Bailey felt sure David's story would tug at her readers' hearts. She just needed to make sure she had some of the key details straight. "The man you're looking for is your mother's brother, correct?"

David nodded. "Yes, ma'am."

"And when do you think he came to Seattle?"

This took them a little while to work out. David remembered his mother telling him she had met his father at their rooming house in the spring of 1901. If Danny's family had first moved west around the time his mother started working at the rooming house, that would have been about two years before, so they probably came to Seattle around 1901, as well.

"And your mother's name was ...?"

"Maude."

"And your uncle was Danny. What was their surname?"

David wasn't sure he understood.

"Well, your surname is Saifert, but your mother

wasn't Maude Saifert when she was a girl, just like your uncle wasn't Danny Embury until he got adopted. Do you know what their family name was?"

David wasn't sure he'd ever heard his mother mention what her name had been before she got married. But then he remembered the stack of letters from his mother's dresser. They'd been addressed to her from before she got married. What had they said on them?

Maude Wilson, he suddenly remembered. "Their family name was Wilson."

Mrs. Bailey smiled. "That's good. That will be an important detail." Then she asked David even more questions about his mother and her brother when they were young. He wasn't able to give her all the answers, but he told her everything he could recall.

"Well, that should be everything I need. With any luck you'll see the story in tomorrow's paper."

And indeed it was there in the Sunday edition:

ORPHANED BOY IN CANADIENS
CAMP NEEDS THE HELP OF *P-I*
READERS
by MADGE BAILEY

As fans of sport in our city know, the Montreal Canadiens are here to battle

our beloved Mets for the Stanley Cup.
The Canadiens, famed wherever hockey
is played as the Flying Frenchmen, are a
battle-scarred team of veterans.

Yet in their camp they have with them
a brave young boy only 14 years old. In
those 14 years he has faced harder hits
than any delivered in a hockey arena.

David Saifert lost his father in the
Great War, one of many thousands
of soldiers from our neighbors to the
north who gave their lives in battle. His
mother and sister lost their lives to the
dreaded Spanish Flu.

David is in Seattle now searching
for the only family he has left. An uncle
he has never known. The brother of
his mother, Maude, an orphan himself,
who came to our city with his adoptive
parents nearly 20 years ago. David
carries a torn photo of his uncle taken
when he was just a boy.

Born Danny Wilson, he became
Danny Embury, or Embree, or perhaps
some other spelling. He may well go
by another name now. If you have any

information about this man, please contact the *Post-Intelligencer* office.

"She did a nice job," Joe said when he read it. "I think you've done all you can do now."

It was time to concentrate on hockey.

CHAPTER 22

Sunday's paper also carried the news of Saturday's second game in the Stanley Cup series. It wasn't just with the sports news. It appeared right on the front page:

LES CANADIENS TAKE SECOND
OF HOCKEY SERIES
Montreal Players Treat Fans to
Sensational Exhibition
by ROYAL BROUGHAM

Grande triomphe pour Les Canadiens! Vive Montreal! The Flying Frenchmen administered a 4–2 spanking to the Seattle hockey team last night and evened up the race for the championship of the world.

Treating the packed Seattle Arena to a sensational exhibition of individual hockey, Newsy Lalonde of the visiting team scored all four of the Montreal goals himself. The eastern champions showed an entire reversal of form over their initial appearance by outskating and outchecking the Mets at every stage of the contest.

From the opening whistle the French team took the jump and the Seattle men could not fathom the stone-wall defense of their opponents. Quick to take advantage of an opening, Montreal was going at a whirlwind clip, while the home crew showed little of their dash from game one.

Les Canadiens played rough hockey last night. They got away with a lot of stuff, and the fans booed the visitors loud and often. Lalonde and his teammates hit hard and used their bodies to stop the rush of the Seattle forwards.

Manager Kennedy was well pleased with his men after the game and predicted they would carry off the big honors now that they have tasted victory.

But once again Mr. Kennedy had spoken too soon. On Monday night it was all Seattle just as in game one. They whipped the Canadiens 7–2. That made it a do-or-die game for the team when they faced the Mets in game four on Wednesday night.

The Canadiens had tried to play it rough in game three. Joe was really throwing his weight around and swinging his stick a little too wildly. It hadn't worked. True, the Mets were getting pretty banged up, but nobody was hurt as badly as Bert Corbeau. He got the worst of it after hitting a Seattle player early in the first period. Corbeau went into him awkwardly and suffered a sprained shoulder. He didn't play at all after that. Billy Couture and Odie Cleghorn, who usually played forward, took turns filling in for him. Joe didn't get any rest at all and had to play the full sixty minutes — except for the two times he took a seat in the penalty box. Newsy Lalonde and Didier Pitre had played the whole game, too.

David had to set up the dressing room pretty much by himself on Wednesday. Al was too busy massaging the players' sore muscles. Everyone had their aches and pains, but only Corbeau's injury was serious. Nobody was sure if he'd be good to go in game four. The newspapers said he probably wouldn't.

"How's he look, Al?" Newsy Lalonde asked as game time approached.

Al made a waggling "so-so" gesture with his hand.

"I'm playing," Corbeau announced. "Don't try and stop me!"

That was what Newsy wanted to hear. "Good. Then Bert's starting on defence with Joe." But Newsy knew he couldn't really count on Corbeau. He'd hoped to start Odie Cleghorn at left wing, but decided he'd better keep Louis Berlinquette there. "Louis will start up front with Didier and me. We'll get you up on the line if we can Odie, but I need you ready to go on defence."

Cleghorn nodded. He'd do whatever was best for the team.

"Okay, boys," Newsy said. "No one needs any fancy words from me. We didn't come three thousand miles to lose to these guys again. Let's show 'em what we're made of!"

Lalonde lined up for the opening faceoff against Frank Foyston. In his striped Seattle sweater, the speedy Mets forward had looked like a blur of red, white, and green so far in the series. He'd scored three of Seattle's seven goals in the first game, gotten one in the 4–2 loss, and then equalled Newsy with four goals of his own in game three. Now he beat Lalonde to the draw in game four, and Seattle went on the attack.

In each of their two lopsided losses, Vézina had given up an early goal. In game three Foyston had beaten him just a little more than a minute after the opening faceoff.

Now Seattle was pressing early again, but Vézina looked more like his usual self.

"Atta boy, Georges!" Cleghorn shouted from the bench as the Canadiens' goalie turned aside a dangerous drive. Jack McDonald and Billy Couture thumped their sticks against the inside of the boards appreciatively. Because the rink was packed with Seattle fans hoping to see their team clinch the Stanley Cup, David and Al were sitting right there on the Canadiens' bench. It was easy for David to see and hear what the players were doing.

Soon Lalonde and Berlinquette had chances for the Canadiens, but Hap Holmes appeared sharp once again in the Seattle net.

"Be nice to get the first one tonight," Cleghorn said.

It turned out that Odie was the first one to get a real good chance.

As play raced from end to end in the opening minutes, it became obvious Corbeau was favouring his shoulder. Newsy sent him off and put Cleghorn on instead. Soon after he got on the ice, Odie rushed forward from the defence and found himself in the clear out front.

Pitre had the puck behind the Mets net, but a Seattle defenceman was on his tail.

"Over here!" Cleghorn shouted.

Pitre spotted him and made a nice pass. Cleghorn snapped his wrists as soon as the puck was on his stick and launched a hard drive that seemed destined for the net ... but Holmes got a glove on the puck and knocked it aside.

Later in the period Lalonde and Pitre fired bullet drives again and again, but Holmes stopped them all. Vézina was matching him save for save in this one, and for the first time all series the game was scoreless after twenty minutes.

David passed out towels in the dressing room so the players could wipe off their sweat. They weren't used to the warm temperatures inside Seattle Arena, and this had been part of their problem during the series. One advantage the Canadiens had over the Mets was that they had three spare players in their lineup and Seattle only had two. Lalonde decided he needed to use the extra player to better benefit.

"We're going to switch up a lot more from now on," he told his teammates during the intermission.

In the second period he kept on swapping Cleghorn and Corbeau. Sometimes he used Cleghorn on the forward line, too. Couture and McDonald saw action, as well, so that Berlinquette and Pitre could get some rest. Through two periods only Newsy had played the full forty minutes. Yet the Canadiens couldn't put the puck past Holmes. At least the Mets hadn't beaten Vézina, either. The game was still scoreless. Despite the

Canadiens' continued line juggling, it remained scoreless through the third period, too.

There was no intermission before the overtime. The break lasted only as long as it took the goalies to change ends. Vézina stopped by the bench for a drink of water and to rinse some of the sweat out of his toque. Although any shot that beat him now would cost his team the Stanley Cup, the Silent Habitant looked as calm as ever. He even winked at David when the boy passed him a towel.

"Continue comme ça, mon Georges!" Newsy said, whacking the goalie on the pads with his stick as he skated for the far end of the rink.

Both teams were tired when they lined up to start overtime. Seattle looked worse, but the Canadiens were showing the strain, too. It didn't appear likely that either team had the stamina to put up much of a defence.

A quick goal seemed inevitable, and the crowd of four thousand was on its feet.

Just as when the game began, Seattle's Frank Foyston won the faceoff and the Mets sped to the attack. Foyston fed the puck to his right winger, Cully Wilson, who shot immediately, but Vézina stopped it. Newsy scooped up the rebound and went end to end with it. He had a good chance, too, but Holmes refused to be beaten.

The teams couldn't keep up such a fast pace, and soon everyone was launching their shots from a long way out. Like tennis players, the goalies kept whacking the puck back and then waiting to see what their opponent could do.

The teams played ten minutes of scoreless overtime hockey, then the goalies switched ends and play started up again. When the timer's whistle blew after ten more minutes had passed, players on both teams collapsed in sheer exhaustion. There was still no score, so it was decided the game should end in a 0–0 tie.

The next day's newspaper summed everything up best:

DRAMATIC CLIMAX TO BATTLE
WHEN MEN DROP TO THE ICE
AFTER FINISH
by ROYAL BROUGHAM

They may be playing for hockey championships for the next thousand years, but they'll never stage a greater struggle than that which held the spectators spellbound last night through the longest scoreless contest in the history of the game.

With both teams struggling until their tongues were hanging out, the throng cheered wildly when some Met skater dashed down the ice on a goal-getting assault and held its breath when Newsy Lalonde or some other Frenchman initiated a charge on the Seattle net.

The crowd waited patiently when the officials were deciding whether the play should continue or not, and when the decision was announced the fans went home perfectly satisfied that they had witnessed a great struggle.

But for all its drama, it was almost as if the game had never happened. It wouldn't have any effect on the series … except for the fact that it had worn people out. Seattle was still a win away from the Stanley Cup, while the Canadiens needed a victory to stay alive. If they got it, the five-game series would have to go to a sixth game.

CHAPTER 23

Neither team went back on the ice during the two days off before Saturday's game. After their marathon struggle on Wednesday, rest was more important than practice. Royal Brougham wrote about all the injuries the teams had suffered in his column on Friday:

THE CASUALTY LIST
by ROYAL BROUGHAM

Here is the list of injured players after the struggle on Wednesday night:

- Jack Walker, Seattle forward, two stitches above eye.
- Louis Berlinquette, Montreal forward, three stitches in lip.
- Frank Foyston, Seattle forward, badly sprained thigh.
- Roy Rickey, Seattle defense, cut across ankle.

- Bobby Rowe, Seattle defense, sprained ankle.
- Bert Corbeau, Montreal defenseman, strained shoulder.

Every other man on both clubs was nursing from one to a half-dozen minor bruises, sprains, and cuts.

The Seattle men were a sorry-looking lot yesterday morning. Several of them did not get out of bed until late in the day and all of them were sore from head to toe.

The Frenchmen, while in better shape, knew they were in a hockey game and several bore marks of the struggle. All of the visitors were dead tired and spent the day resting.

Al was kept busy on Thursday and Friday changing bandages on cuts and massaging muscles. For David there were holes to repair in the elbows of sweaters and knees of socks. But fixing them didn't take all of his time. Although it was often raining, David went out when the weather wasn't too bad. He walked the streets and peered at men's faces, still hoping to spot a man who looked like him. On Friday he visited Mr. Embree's office again, but Miss Carter told him that none of the other families had been able to provide any information. On Saturday morning David went across the street to see Mrs. Bailey at the newspaper office.

"We've been getting telephone calls and letters," she told him, "but they're mostly from people who just want to wish you good luck. Several callers claimed to be your uncle." Mrs. Bailey saw the flash of excitement in David's eyes. "But they couldn't even answer the simplest questions based on the things you were able to tell me."

David slumped in his seat.

"Still, there was one call that seems promising. I wasn't going to tell you about it until I had a chance to find out more, but there was a gentleman who called to say that he rents a room from a man named Daniel Williams. He has no idea if Mr. Williams was an orphan, but he said they'd been talking about the Stanley Cup series and Mr. Williams mentioned he had grown up in Montreal and moved west with his parents as a young man."

David sat up straight. There was excitement in his eyes again, but then a look of doubt. "So why didn't *he* call?"

"Well, the gentleman explained that Mr. Williams and his wife were called out of town last Saturday morning. They never saw the Sunday paper. They've been in Portland all this week, where Mrs. Williams's mother has taken ill. However, they're due back in town on the late train this evening. Our telephone caller has promised to speak with him when he sees him tomorrow and to call the newspaper office on Monday to let us know."

But if the Canadiens lost on Saturday night, they'd be leaving Seattle to go to Victoria at nine o'clock on Monday morning.

Mrs. Bailey promised David that she'd send a telegram to him at the team's hotel in Victoria if they'd already left before she heard anything. So as if he needed any more reasons, this was another good one for hoping the Canadiens could pull off a win that evening. But the team got off to another bad start.

Despite their many injuries — or maybe because of them — the Mets wanted to take care of business quickly. With another full house of four thousand fans screaming their support, the Seattle speedsters came out flying. The Canadiens stood their ground, hoping the Mets would tire themselves out. Vézina made a few good saves, but Frank Foyston found the net at 5:40 of the first period. He'd picked the puck up from a scramble in front and beat the Montreal goalie with a quick shot to the far corner.

Immediately, Newsy called in two of his substitutes. "Cleghorn for Corbeau," the captain ordered. "Berlinquette for Couture."

For the next nine minutes no one scored, but the Mets had the better of the play. Then Jack Walker scooped up the puck near centre ice. He zigzagged through the Canadiens' defence and beat Vézina to make the score 2–0. That was how the first period ended, but just 1:18 after the intermission Walker scored again and Seattle led 3–0.

Both teams switched their players often during the second period, and the extra man the Canadiens were carrying started to make a difference. Pitre and Lalonde were pouring it on, but Holmes was having another great game. Nothing got past him, and the score was still 3–0 Seattle when the second period ended. The Mets' fans cheered their team off the ice, certain they were twenty minutes away from becoming Stanley Cup champions.

The mood inside the Canadiens' dressing room was surprisingly upbeat.

"It's okay, boys! It's okay!" Cleghorn kept saying over and over as David passed out the towels. "The tide's turning. It's going our way. We just gotta get that first one!"

"Odie's right!" Couture hollered. "We get one, we're gonna get a bunch. You can feel it!"

There were similar expressions of confidence from most of the players around the room. Vézina was his usual silent self, but that was what everyone expected. They would have been worried if he suddenly started getting excited. Corbeau wasn't yelling much, either, but he looked as if he couldn't wait to get back out there as Al re-taped the wrap on his injured shoulder. Only Joe seemed unusually quiet. He was pale, too. Pitre had dropped back on defence to take his spot during the second period, and Joe hadn't returned to the ice after that.

"You all right?" David asked him.

Joe glanced up. His eyes seemed glassy. "I'll be okay. Just need some more rest." He smiled weakly. "I'm not as young as I used to be."

But it was obvious that ten minutes in the dressing room wasn't enough time for him. Joe was worn out, and Newsy could see that his old rival was in no condition to go back on the ice. "Didier," the captain said, "you'll keep playing with Bert on defence. Odie, I want you up front with me. You, too, Billy."

Newsy looked around the dressing room. He liked what he saw in his teammates' eyes. "Okay, boys," he said after a moment, "let's go."

———————

Newsy beat Foyston for the opening faceoff, and the Canadiens poured into the Seattle end. They kept the pressure on but still couldn't put the puck past Holmes. The Mets had their share of chances, too, but Vézina turned every shot aside. Then Couture picked up the puck deep in the Canadiens' zone.

Couture usually played defence, but Newsy had been using him on the wing a lot in the series. He hadn't added much scoring punch, but he'd been using his size to advantage against the smaller Mets defencemen. Now he showed his skillful side, too. Couture raced from end to end, stickhandling neatly into the Seattle zone. Then he zipped the puck across the ice for Cleghorn ... and Odie scored!

Seattle 3, Montreal 1.

Newsy mussed Odie's hair with a gloved hand. He tapped Couture on the butt with his stick. "Nice work. Now take a break."

Berlinquette replaced Couture and lined up for the faceoff on Lalonde's left. Cleghorn remained on the right wing. Again Newsy won the draw, and the three Canadiens forwards sped to the attack. Using Odie as a decoy, Newsy slipped a nice pass over to Berlinquette. Louis stepped around Roy Rickey on the Seattle defence, then froze Bobby Rowe with a quick pass back to Newsy. The captain snagged the puck and moved in on Holmes. Faking one way, then moving the other, Newsy fooled the goalie again. Just one minute later the team had another mark on the scoreboard.

Seattle 3, Montreal 2.

"Told ya!" Couture shouted on the bench. "They're gonna start coming in bunches now!"

But the scoring stopped after that. Both teams had plenty of chances, but Holmes and Vézina matched each other save for save.

Time was running out when Newsy led another assault on the Seattle end. The Canadiens were buzzing around the net, but Holmes kept the puck out. He made a tough save on one sizzling shot, and the rebound went straight up in the air. Newsy reached as high as he could and knocked the puck down with his glove. As it was falling, he swung his stick like a baseball bat and swatted the falling disk into the net.

The score was tied 3–3. The Mets' lead was gone. Their fans were stunned.

With only three minutes left to play neither team wanted to see overtime again. Both sides went at it hard for the winning goal, but Holmes and Vézina refused to be beaten. The score was still tied when the timer sounded his whistle to end the third period.

The league officials in charge of the Stanley Cup series had decided that if any more games went into overtime, they would be played to the finish no matter how long it took. It seemed impossible that the game's fast pace could be kept up beyond sixty minutes, but this one raced on and on again with no end in sight. The Mets had some good chances early, but Vézina stopped them. When the play started going the Canadiens' way,

Holmes staved off defeat with save after save.

Finally, after fifteen minutes, the Canadiens got a break. The blade broke on one of Walker's skates and he had to go off for repairs. Then Foyston took a hit on his wounded thigh and collapsed in pain. He struggled off the ice, and Seattle suddenly found itself missing its two best players. Even worse, the Mets had no substitutes left they could use, so when Cully Wilson came to the bench gasping for breath, there was no one to go on in his place. Wilson had to stay out there.

Like everyone else in the rink, David was up on his feet. From where he stood at the Canadiens' bench, he was the first one to see the confusion on the Seattle side. Jack McDonald spotted it, too.

McDonald hadn't seen any action for the Canadiens since the end of the third period, but he'd come onto the ice just a short while before Foyston got hurt. He was the freshest man in the game, and he sprung into action. McDonald scooped up the loose puck and steamed into the Seattle end. He split the defence of Rowe and Rickey, then moved in alone on Holmes. McDonald snapped a quick shot on goal and scored!

The Canadiens won the game 4–3. The comeback was complete.

The team was still alive ... and so were David's chances of finding his uncle.

CHAPTER 24

Joe Hall had a fever, and it was a pretty high one. David was worried. How could he be anything else after what he'd been through with the flu in the fall? But no one else seemed to think Joe's fever was cause for much concern. Not even Dr. Stephens, who was called in to examine him on Sunday morning.

"It's just exhaustion," the doctor said. "Nothing more. He'll be fine when he gets some rest. From what I hear," he added with a shake of his head, "it's amazing they haven't all keeled over after the way they've played these last two games."

In fact, Cully Wilson had collapsed on the ice after Jack McDonald's winning goal. His teammates had to carry him back to the Seattle dressing room. Wilson was running a fever, too.

At least the teams had two more days off before the final game. Mr. Kennedy and Pete Muldoon agreed to wait until Tuesday to play it. That would be April 1. It seemed unlikely that Joe would be ready to play by then, but everyone knew he would if he could. For now, though, he needed rest.

With nothing really to do on Sunday and the weather rainy again, David decided to go out at noon and see a movie. There were several theatres in the area, and he walked up to the Colonial. It was a block north of the hotel on Fourth Avenue where Westlake cut between Pike and Pine. It was one of those triangle-shaped intersections, and the Plaza Hotel stood in the middle like the bow of a giant ship.

A lot of the hockey players had spent their free time around this area during the team's stay in Seattle. There were several restaurants there, as well as Greenland Billiards, where some of them liked to shoot pool. The Colonial Theatre had a tall sign out front that stood well above any of the other signs on the street. That made it easy to spot.

For the price of a dime, David watched two movies. The first was a comedy called *Society Stuff* with Alice Howell. The second film was *Never Say Quit*. It starred George Walsh. The sign out front said it was "a comedy full of tough luck and laughs." It was pretty funny, and lots of people in the theatre were laughing, but David actually found it a little bit sad. In a strange way the story reminded him of his own situation.

George Walsh plays a man named Reginald Jones. He has thirteen letters in his name and was born on Friday the thirteenth in a house on 113th Street. Naturally, bad luck follows him around. Reginald loses all his money in the stock market, but then finds out he's going to inherit a fortune from his aunt — provided he can make it to her funeral on time. It seems easy enough, but on his way, Reginald gets tricked by some con men and winds up missing it. When he arrives too late, his uncle throws him out.

Desperate for money, Reginald takes a job working on a ship. Turns out, though, that the ship is being run by pirates ... or a gang of crooks, anyway. They have plans to kidnap the old professor who's travelling onboard with his daughter. In the end, things turn out all right for Reginald. He fights the crooks with his flying fists, rescues the professor, and even gets the girl.

And they all live happily ever after.

David wondered if his own story was going to end that way or not.

———————————

The man at the front desk was watching for David when he got back to the hotel. "There's a message for you." He handed David an envelope.

David tore it open eagerly and pulled out the piece of paper inside.

David,

I can wait at my desk until 3:30. If you're back by then, please come and see me. I think it's good news!
— Madge Bailey
P.S. Bring your photo.

"What time is it?" David asked the man at the desk.

"Ten past three."

"Thank you!" David cried over his shoulder as he turned and ran for the stairs. He went up to his room and got the photograph, then raced back down and across the street.

Madge Bailey was smiling when she saw him running toward her desk a few minutes later. "I think it's him."

David didn't need to ask who.

"Daniel Williams telephoned me at home a little past noon. He told me his name had been Danny Wilson when he was a boy and that he was adopted by Gerald and Stella Embury. They left Montreal in 1899 and came to Seattle in 1902. His mother remarried after his father died. That's why his name isn't Embury anymore."

That was just what Joe had suspected, yet the rest of the pieces fitted David's story almost perfectly. In fact, Mrs. Bailey had wondered if they fitted too perfectly.

"A lot of that information," she said, "was already in

my story about you. And most of what wasn't he could have guessed at and simply made up. For now we have no way to prove he's telling the truth. And he didn't seem to remember a lot of the things you told me about, but he claims to have the other half of your photo."

"Really!" David said excitedly. "Where does he live? When can I see him?"

Mrs. Bailey glanced at the clock on the wall. It was nearly 3:30. She was supposed to go home, but the reporter in her needed to know how the story would end. Besides, there was no way she was going to make David wait another day. "I'll telephone Mr. Williams right now. If he's home, we'll go straight away."

"No need for that," a voice behind them said.

They turned around with a start. A man was walking up to Mrs. Bailey's desk, and he looked so much like an older version of David that she gasped when she saw him.

David just stared. "Uncle Danny?" he finally said. His voice was barely a whisper.

The man's head tilted a bit when he smiled. "No one's ever called me that before." Then Daniel Williams reached into a pocket inside his coat. He took something out and put it on Mrs. Bailey's desk. It was a photograph of a teenage girl. Or rather, it was half a photograph.

David put his own photo down beside it. The edges of both had been rubbed too smooth to say they fitted together like pieces of a puzzle, but there was no doubt at all they were a perfect match.

"I've been looking at it all these years," Daniel said, "and wondering if she was doing the same."

"She was," David said. "She looked at it a lot. And she kept all your letters, too. But why did you stop writing to her?"

David had never seen a grown man cry before, but there were tears in his uncle's eyes now. "I was still just a boy. Not much older than you are now. I loved my stepfather very much. I'd already lost so many people, and after he passed away, I decided I didn't want to be that close to anyone anymore. So I stopped answering Maude's letters ... and after a while she stopped writing, too. But I couldn't forget her."

Daniel wiped the tears from his eyes. Then he shook his head. "I never even knew she had a son."

"And a daughter, too," David told him. "The first time she ever showed me your picture was a little while after my sister was born. She said that Alice liked to cry and that you did, too, when you were a baby."

Daniel laughed. "I don't remember that."

"I used to think I hated my sister," David said, "but my mother always said there's nothing in life as important as family. She was right, and I know that's why she wanted me to find you."

"And now you have. And you can stay here with me and my wife. We'll be your family now. We are your family."

CHAPTER 25

David couldn't wait to tell Joe the good news. But when he got back to the hotel, he knew right away something was wrong. Dr. Stephens was talking to Al in the hallway outside Joe's room. And both of them were wearing masks.

"We're being careful," Al told David. "It might still be nothing. It's too soon to tell, but Jack McDonald's got a fever now, too."

"Is it all right to see Joe? I have something to tell him."

"Now's probably not the best time," the doctor said. "He needs to sleep. Hopefully, we'll know more in the morning."

When Monday morning came, nobody was any surer of anything. The newspapers were still filled with stories about Saturday's game and the winner-take-all final that was scheduled for Tuesday. There was a lot of news about everybody's cuts and bruises and who on which team was hurt worse than whom. Royal Brougham spent most of his column explaining how much weight the Seattle players had sweated off during the series. He didn't say much about the Canadiens. Mostly that Corbeau's shoulder was still bad. He also mentioned that Lalonde "had a number of bumps" and that Pitre "has some bruises on his legs that will keep him from going at top speed." All he said about Joe and Jack McDonald was that their high fevers were "caused by their exertion in the last two battles." There was still nobody who seemed very concerned: "Both teams are a weary-looking bunch, but neither squad lacks the determination to win the final game. The managers both say their players will go all out to win tomorrow at all costs."

On Monday night all that changed. Mr. Kennedy developed a fever. So did Newsy. Louis Berlinquette and Billy Couture had fevers, too. It was obvious now that it wasn't just fatigue making people sick. It was something worse. Much worse. The Spanish Flu was back!

No one was thinking of the Stanley Cup now. With five of their nine players too sick even to get out of bed on Tuesday morning, there was no way the Canadiens would be able to play that night. And even if they somehow could, there was no way that city officials in Seattle were going to let four thousand people jam together inside Seattle Arena. It would be much too dangerous to have so many people exposed to the germs. So at 2:30 on Tuesday afternoon a decision was made. The final game of the series was cancelled. There would be no Stanley Cup champion in 1919.

The bonus money the players had been so worried about was going to be split fifty/fifty by the two teams. Every player on each side would receive $262.70. It was good money, but it was no longer so important. Suddenly, a battle that had seemed like a life-and-death struggle had truly become one.

Nurses were sent to the Georgian Hotel on Tuesday afternoon so that the sick Canadiens could be treated in their beds. The newer cases all had temperatures of around 101 degrees. They were certainly high, though not considered life-threatening ... unless they went up instead of down. Joe and Jack McDonald were already in dangerous territory. Their fevers had crept over 104 degrees. They needed more treatment than they could get in a hotel room, so Dr. Stephens sent for an ambulance to take them to Providence Hospital.

The hospital was close to the team's hotel. Al agreed to take David there on Wednesday afternoon.

"How they doing, Doc?" Al asked when they saw Stephens.

"Not much change, I'm afraid. Mr. McDonald's fever has come down a bit today but Mr. Hall's is still over 104. If it doesn't come down soon, we're going to lose him."

"Joe's a fighter," Al told him. "Toughest hockey

player I've ever seen."

"Well, I'm afraid he's in the fight of his life right now."

"Is there any chance the kid and I can see him?"

"I'm not sure that would be wise."

"But he's got news that Joe will want to hear. Couldn't good news help him get better?"

The doctor considered that for a moment. "I suppose it's worth a try. Were you by any chance sick in the fall when all this started up?"

"Not me, Doc," Al said. "I've been fit as a fiddle."

Dr. Stephens glanced at David. "What about you?"

"I had the flu in November."

"A bad case or mild?"

"Bad, I guess. I was in bed for nearly a month."

The doctor nodded. If David's body had already fought off the Spanish Flu, then he was unlikely to catch it again. "The boy can see him, but I think it might be too dangerous for you."

David was nervous when he entered Joe's room. He hadn't seen his mother or his sister when they were sick. He didn't really know what a flu victim looked like. Would Joe's skin be blue? Would there be blood oozing from his nose or mouth? The doctor probably wouldn't have let him in if Joe's condition was that bad. Still, the sight of him was startling.

Joe was lying in bed, but he was propped up so that his head and chest weren't lying flat. His skin wasn't blue, but it was chalky white. It seemed to be pulled too tight across his forehead, and his cheeks were sunken and hollow. His short dark hair was greasy and plastered to his scalp with sweat. His eyes were open, but they didn't seem to see anything he was looking at. And his breath came in huffs as if it were being squeezed out of his lungs by some kind of machine.

"Joe? Can you hear me? Joe? It's David."

At first there was no reaction, then Joe slowly lifted his head off the pillow. David saw his eyes begin to focus.

"I found him, Joe. I found my uncle. We found him, really. It was the story in the newspaper that did it."

David noticed Joe nod slightly, and there was a thin smile on his face when he rested his head back on the pillow. Then he waggled his hand a little as if he were trying to muss David's hair. The effort of even that small gesture exhausted him, and he fell asleep. David sat beside Joe's bed a few minutes longer, then left. He knew there was nothing more he could do for Joe. All anyone could do was wait and see.

———————

Now that the Stanley Cup series was cancelled, the newspapers that had followed the games with interest filled their pages with medical updates instead:

> Seattle, April 3 — Word that George Kennedy was seriously ill this morning was later denied by his nurse. She asserts that he is recovering more rapidly than could be expected.

> Louis Berlinquette and Newsy Lalonde are on the mend, but sympathy should be extended to Jack McDonald, Billy Couture, and Joe Hall. These three boys are still dangerously ill. Odie Cleghorn of the Canadiens is the latest of the easterners to be stricken with the influenza.

> Seattle, April 4 — Three members of the Seattle team, Roy Rickey, Muzz Murray, and Manager Pete Muldoon yesterday became sick. All three are under the care of a physician.

> Word from the Montreal camp is that there is great improvement in the condition of George Kennedy. He will soon be out of bed. Couture,

Berlinquette, McDonald, and Lalonde are on the mend, too. McDonald and Couture both had serious attacks, but they are recuperating rapidly.

Joe Hall remains in critical condition. He has been moved to Columbus Sanitarium.

Seattle, April 5 — George Kennedy and Newsy Lalonde are expected to get out of bed today for a short time at least. Berlinquette is improving rapidly and expects to exercise a little this afternoon in his room.

Jack McDonald, whose condition was serious, is reported as gaining and it is now thought he is out of danger. Seattle's Pete Muldoon is holding his own, while Roy Rickey made big gains during the past 24 hours and Muzz Murray is not considered in dangerous condition.

All the hockey players except Joe Hall are improving. The Canadiens defenseman's

condition is reported as being serious. A
case of pneumonia has developed and he
is in critical shape.

It didn't seem fair. Just as David finally found a family
to belong to again, he lost someone else. Joe Hall died
in the Columbus Sanitarium at 2:30 in the afternoon on
Saturday April 5, 1919. His funeral was held three days
later in Vancouver. Joe's mother, a brother, and a few
other relatives lived in that city, and his wife and children
were going to move there, too, so they could be close to
the rest of their family.

David went to Vancouver, as well. His Uncle Danny
took him there to attend the funeral. He hadn't been
able to say a proper goodbye to his parents or sister. At
least he was there to say one to Joe. He saw his children
and told them how much their father had missed them
when he was away, and what a good man "Bad Joe"
really was, and that he would never forget him.

At least he could do that for his friend.

ACKNOWLEDGEMENTS

First, thank you to Michael Carroll and Dundurn Press for the opportunity to write fiction again. While there were times I worried I couldn't do it anymore, working on this book was mostly a lot of fun!

Even though this book is a work of fiction, it is based on a lot of real-life events. George Kennedy, Joe Hall, Newsy Lalonde, and the rest of the Montreal Canadiens were real people. So were the Seattle hockey players and newspaper reporters. Even Benton Embree, who helps David in his search, really was a lawyer in Seattle. Although I've used them all fictitiously, much effort was taken to present the historical details pertaining to their lives and time period as accurately as possible.

There are many people to whom I wish to express my thanks; first among them is my mother-in-law, Alice Embury. Alice grew up in Montreal, and though she was a girl about David's age in the 1920s and 1930s, her memories, and the stories she has written down, gave me all the details I needed to create David's neighbourhood near Papineau Avenue. In fact, Alice was born in the house on Chabot Street I used for David's home. (Although the address was 1960 in the 1910s, a switch in the numbering system in the 1920s changed it to 5628, which it remains to this day.) I gave David's sister Alice's name in tribute and used the Embury name for the same reason.

The Montefiore Home where David is taken during the Spanish Flu epidemic was a real place in Montreal, though it didn't actually open until a few years later. Judy Gordon has written two very interesting books about the Montreal Hebrew Orphans' Home, which opened in 1909, and the Montefiore Hebrew Orphans' Home. Judy's husband, Myer Gordon, lived at the Montefiore Home in the 1920s and 1930s, and between Judy's books and the willingness of both of them to answer my questions, it seemed the perfect place for David. Not everything I wrote may be entirely accurate, but any changes were made for the sake of the story and are my responsibility.

My own French isn't very good — in fact, almost non-existent — so I'm most thankful to Jean-Patrice Martel for providing me with French translations and proper phrases for the French characters in the book. The funny thing is, I had already named a key character J-P after Jean-Patrice before I even thought to ask him for his help! Jean-Patrice is a colleague with the Society for International Hockey Research (SIHR), and there are many other SIHR members who helped, either directly or indirectly, with bits of research for this story. Among them are Ernie Fitzsimmons, Paul Kitchen, Bill Sproule, and Jason Wilson.

Craig Campbell and Phil Pritchard at the Hockey Hall of Fame have always been very helpful to me, and in this case I must thank Craig especially for showing me Joe Hall's scrapbook in the Hall of Fame's resource centre and for introducing me to Larry Hall, the grandson of "Bad Joe" himself. As it turns out, Larry and I are practically neighbours!

Another person who deserves a huge "assist" for her help in researching this novel is Jo-Anne Colby of the CP Archives. Jo-Anne provided invaluable information about the trains, routes, and ferry schedules that would have taken the Canadiens to Seattle in 1919. Although I changed their voyage a little bit — the Canadiens actually stopped to play exhibition games in Regina and Calgary en route west — this was again done for the sake of the story. Dona Bubelis and the Magazine and Newspaper Department of the Seattle Public Library were most helpful, as well. I was very impressed with their online service.

Finally, I would like to thank my wife, Barbara. Her support and encouragement are never-ending.

SELECTED READING AND WEBSITES

BOOKS

Barry, John M. *The Great Influenza: The Epic Story of the Deadliest Plague in History*. New York: Penguin, 2004.

Coleman, Charles C. *The Trail of the Stanley Cup: Volume 1 1893–1926*. Toronto: National Hockey League, 1966.

Diamond, Dan et al. *Total Hockey: The Official Encyclopedia of the National Hockey League Volume 2*. Kingston, NY: Total Sports Publishing, 2000.

____. *Total NHL: The Ultimate Source on the National Hockey League*. Toronto: Dan Diamond and Associates, 2003.

Fischler, Stan, and Shirley Fischler. *Heroes and History: Voices from the NHL's Past!* Toronto: McGraw-Hill Ryerson, 1994.

Getz, David. *Purple Death: The Mysterious Flu of 1918*. New York: Henry Holt and Company, 2000.

Gordon, Judy. *Four Hundred Brothers and Sisters: The Story of Two Jewish Orphanages in Montreal*. Toronto: MJ Publications, 2002.

_____. *Four Hundred Brothers and Sisters: Their Story Continues ...* Toronto: MJ Publications, 2004.

Iezzoni, Lynette. *Influenza 1918: The Worst Epidemic in American History*. New York: TV Books LLC, 1999.

Jenish, D'Arcy. *The Montreal Canadiens: 100 Years of Glory*. Toronto: Doubleday Canada, 2008.

Krohn, Katherine. *The 1918 Flu Pandemic*. Mankato, MN: Coughlan Publishing, 2007.

Pettigrew, Eileen. *The Silent Enemy: Canada and the Deadly Flu of 1918*. Saskatoon: Western Producer Prairie Books, 1983.

WEBSITES

Bibliothèque et Archives nationals Québec, Collections: *www.banq.qc.ca/portal/dt/collections/ collections.jsp*. Digital collections allow searches of old newspapers and street guides.

Canadian Pacific Railway: *www8.cpr.ca/cms/English/ General+Public/Heritage/default.htm*. An online history of the CPR.

Hockey Hall of Fame: *www.hhof.com*. The official website of the Hockey Hall of Fame.

Hockey-Reference.com: *www.hockey-reference.com*. A statistical database of every player in NHL history.

Joe Hall: *www.legendsofhockey.net/LegendsOfHockey/ jsp/LegendsMember.jsp?type=Player&mem=P1961 05&list=ByName#photo*. Joe Hall's page features a biography, his statistics, and photos.

Judaism: *http://judaism.about.com*. This comprehensive guide to Judaism gives great detail and insight into rituals, beliefs, and holidays.

"The Killer Flu Pandemic of 1918": *www.life.com/ image/first/in-gallery/25771/the-killer-flu-pandemic-of-1918*. This high-quality yet heartbreaking slide show features beautiful photos from the flu pandemic of 1918 and photos showing similar effects from the 2009 epidemic.

Montreal Canadiens: *http://canadiens.nhl.com*. The official website of the Montreal Canadiens, including photos, statistics, and history.

Museum of History and Industry: *www.seattlehistory. org*. An online history of Seattle and a photo archive.

National Hockey League: *www.nhl.com*. The official website of the NHL features an extensive archive of players and teams, as well as current information on favourite players.

Newspaper Archive: *www.newspaperarchive.com*. Search old newspaper articles online.

Seattle Public Library: *www.spl.org*. Emails with research questions are answered promptly.

Society for International Hockey Research: *www. sihrhockey.org.* A huge database of information and hockey statistics for members of the Society for International Hockey Research.

Stanley Cup Championship (1919): *www. mbhockeyhalloffame.ca/asset_library/history/1919_ StanleyCupChampionship.pdf.* A fantastic article with all you need to know about the 1919 Stanley Cup Championship and how it was affected by the Spanish Flu.

Toronto Public Library: *www.torontopubliclibrary.ca.* Find articles in magazines, newspapers, and more.